SEX
MAGIC
FOOD

SEX
MAGIC
FOOD

Amiya Cleveland

YEMAYA, LLC
GRAND PRAIRIE, TX

To my husband Tytus, my Papa Legba. You are forever my gentleman.

Acknowledgements

I'd like to give thanks to my husband, Tytus, for helping me to imagine.

To my brother, Jerrod, thank you for being my biggest cheer-leader.

To my cousin, Kay, thank you for bringing out the fire in me!

To my friend Shun, thank you for inspiring me to heal through writing.

To my assistant, Dahlia, thank you for covering my store, which allowed me to create.

To my Editor, Angie Ransome-Jones, thank you for guiding me through the process.

To Genice Johnson, thank you for your impeccable attention to detail.

Yemaya, Ase.
Oshun, Ase.
Oya, Ase.
Esu, Ase.
Olodumare, Ase.

Contents

Chapter 1

"Children shouldn't be created from situations like this. It puts something deep inside of them, almost like karma that must be worked out for itself.

My pretty little girl, Sheela. With piercing brown eyes, butterscotch skin, and hair like fresh cotton. She is only in the third grade, but I can already feel the question in her spirit.

"Momma, how come I can't have a Daddy?"

It was different in the 60s; I never expected it to be like this. I realize it was wrong to have a baby with a married man, but I lived in the fantasy of free love and drugs, not recognizing its eventual inflated cost. A cost I also destined my precious girl to pay.

I can tell my momma's disappointed that I brought Sheela into this. She's been hard on me for choosing this life. But being a black woman, in Texas, in 1975, doesn't lend much to your monthly pay unless you're willing to give up some "johnson". Thank God Momma's willing to hold Sheela for tonight. I need my gentlemen, and my magic makes sure they need me. I'll do anything to take care of my baby; she's all I got.

"Get comfortable Marvin, it's almost ready." Sadie instructs the tall and muscular man waiting in her bedroom.

She knows Marvin's listening, as she hears the familiar metal clinking sound from his belt buckle.

In the kitchen, Sadie pays attention to butter boiling in a shallow pot as she adds a sachet of crushed cannabis leaves.

Steam rises from another pot as she boils sweet milk to a thick foam.

Sadie lowers the flame before she pours honey into a cup. Adding the herbed butter, she stirs with a copper spoon before pouring the hot milk over top. Letting the drink cool a little before taking a sip to make sure everything is as it should be. Satisfied, she sets the warm love potion on the tray.

Her deep brown skin reflects the full moonlight as she walks toward Marvin. The satin fabric of her short leopard print robe scrapes the blanketed floor as she sits.

Steam rises from the lonely cup of cream and honey artfully arranged on the tray next to her. Sadie rests against her elbows, making eye contact with Marvin and asking him to join her.

Marvin crawls to meet Sadie. They both sit, facing each other, smiling, and enjoying the notable contrast of their complexions.

"Please tell me what you need." Sadie gently directs.

Marvin responds, "I want to feel loved. I want to feel sexy. I want to be fed."

As he assumes his position, Sadie faces him, expelling her warm breath, as she seductively places her hands against his thighs.

Sitting with crossed legs, they stare at each other. Sadie slowly rises, kissing Marvin around his face and on his shoulders. She takes her kisses across the torso and onto his back. Speaking over him, Sadie appeases Marvin, telling him he is sexy and will be fed.

She grabs his face, moving closer to him and straddling his waist, gripping it with her folded legs. Sadie's hands move gently over Marvin's broad shoulders as she places her arms around his neck. Squeezing him tightly, their hearts beat together as their genitals touch, pulsing in unison.

Grabbing the sweet milk from the tray. Sadie holds the cup to Marvin's mouth as the liquid flows through his lips. Heavy cream and honey drips down his neck and onto his chest.

"What's this flavor?"

"It's indica. It will help your mind relax."

Marvin nods his head, continuing to drink the brewed cream.

Sadie wipes the drips from his lips and places the cup to the side while looking deep into Marvin's eyes.

"Are you still hungry?"

"Yes" Marvin acknowledges as he grips the sheer white canopy that surrounds the blankets.

Feeling satisfied that Marvin's desire is insatiable, Sadie reclines back onto the floor, places her fingers inside the cup of cream and rubs them across Marvin's lips.

"Lick it." Sadie commands.

Marvin submits, gliding his tongue across his full wet lips.

Sadie spreads her legs and Marvin asks for permission to enter her. His manhood stands erect as she allows him to slip inside.

Marvin moans, his body quivering as he makes love to her. Tasting the herbed cream on his lips, his eyes roll to the back of his head.

Marvin begs with parting lips, anticipating the next taste. "Give me some more."

Sadie submerges her fingers into the cup. She gently releases the flavors into his mouth. His tongue circles around her fingers as he chases the drips of cream down her arm.

Entranced, Marvin picks up the cup and pours the elixir over Sadie's body, pooling it into her navel before pulling back and using it to sweeten the water between her thighs. Preparing herself for pleasure, Sadie points her toes into the carpet, bracing her full figure in place as her elbows press firmly into the ground.

Her head tilted back, Sadie moans as Marvin's lips glide across the curves of her body. Stopping over her navel, Marvin sucks the sweet cream from inside. Sadie's body convulses as he continues below her waist, using his tongue to stroke up and down, circling and sucking. Sadie rises to orgasm as her legs collapse, too weak to hold a stable position.

"You want me to drown in this sweet water don't you?" Marvin playfully insinuates.

Raising his body, Marvin grips her thighs, bringing his moans in sequence as he slides inside her, thrusting back and forth. Sadie pants heavily as she resumes her position; her body held firmly in place by tipped fingers and pointed toes.

"My little sex doll."

Marvin lifts Sadie's legs from the ground and places her toes in his mouth. Feasting until his fetish is satisfied.

Her feet fall back to the ground as Marvin slides his hands under her ass, and lifts her from the ground. Their bodies seem to merge as he thrusts faster. Overcome with ecstasy, Marvin threatens to faint as the tender grip of her body strokes him up and down. A primal wail escapes his lungs and passion drains from his body as he cums inside her.

Appeased, Sadie retreats to her bathroom. She returns lighting the wick of a yellow candle. Whispering a spell into the flame, Sadie places the candle on her altar.

"I enjoyed you Marvin, but you better get going now. Your wife may miss you."

Sadie directs Marvin, wrapping the satin robe around her body.

"I love you, Sadie. Let me stay with you."

"Now you know that's not the deal, Marvin. Your love is for Jane Marie. I want you to be happy, but with her. We'll get together in 28 days."

Sadie winks, but is firm as she walks toward the front door.

"That's bullshit, I can't keep waiting a month to be with you. Who else are you with besides me?"

Marvin grabs Sadie, pulling her into a tight hug and then clutching her shoulders to stare into her eyes.

"Let's not go there."

Sadie pushes away, leading Marvin to the exit door.

"What the fuck do you mean, Sadie? Come here and let me talk to you for a minute."

Marvin forcefully grips the back of Sadie's neck to guide her back toward the bedroom.

"Get your hands off me, mutha fucka!"

Sadie quickly reaches to remove Marvin's hand from her neck.

Slapping her hand, Marvin tightens his grip, causing Sadie to scream and wince in pain. His beige skin reveals pink flesh as she swings and claws at him, fighting to free herself. Briefly out of his grip, Sadie stumbles to a stance and reaches for a crystal vase filled with yellow roses. But before she can use the weapon, pain fills her head as Marvin pulls her thick curly hair and uses it to swing her forcefully to the ground.

The silk robe opens, exposing Sadie's naked body as Marvin drags her kicking and screaming into the bedroom.

"You're going too far! Stop it, Marvin! Please!"

Sadie cries out, screaming in tears as the hair rips from her scalp.

Marvin throws Sadie onto the blanketed floor to adjust his dropping pants as she scrambles away. Stumbling to stand, Sadie runs into the bathroom and locks the door.

"Go away, Marvin! I never want to see you again! You're fucking dead to me!"

Sadie sobs, screaming at him through the locked door.

"Is that so?"

Marvin takes his belt and wraps it around the bathroom doorknob, fastening the other end to her heavy wooden dresser located next to the door to prevent Sadie from escaping.

Lifting the yellow candle from Sadie's altar, Marvin uses it to light the sheer canopy that dangles from the ceiling. Smoke enters the bathroom and burns through Sadie's nostrils as she pulls and bangs on the door, screaming and begging for her life.

"Let me out! Please Marvin, don't do this! Please don't take me from our baby!"

"Maybe she's better without you. We'll see."

Marvin cold-heartedly tosses the candle onto the blanketed floor before escaping from the house.

Fire leaps from the draped fabrics and quickly climbs the walls. The heavy wooden dresser crackles with embers as the bathroom door grows hot, burning Sadie's hands while she screams in terror. Submitting to her fate, Sadie's skin blisters as smoke and fire painfully embrace her body. Life leaves Sadie's eyes as she moans for Sheela.

Chapter 2

My ears mute the sounds of praise in the sanctuary as my eyes follow the dapperly dressed brothers of the church. I'm intoxicated by the scent of their masculine colognes and I'm starting to feel a familiar tingle between my legs. It's a shame that not one of them will risk my grandmother's wrath to ask me out. Or, maybe they can tell I'm a weird 21-year-old virgin.

The air in the sanctuary feels thick with energy and the people of the church are standing with their hands reached out towards the heavens, crying and thanking God. The floor vibrates as the congregation dances in praise.

"For we all have sinned and fallen short of the Glory of God."

Pastor Webb recites from his Bible while patting his brow and questioning the congregation.

"But, brothers and sisters, children of God, why are we tempted to sin?"

He looks out among the people, but stares only at me.

I nervously run my fingers along the red threads of the cushioned pews and look away as my heart rate increases.

"Sheela Diggs! Pay attention to your Word" my grandmother sternly announces as she glares at me over the frame of her spectacles.

"Yes Grandmother." I whisper, correcting my posture and opening my Bible.

My momma's leather bookmark falls onto the space next to me. Lifting it, I imagine how she would look now. I haven't seen my momma in almost 11 years; not since I was in the third grade.

"Glory! Glory! And let the church say Amen!" roars Pastor Webb.

Wrapping up the sermon and wiping his face, Pastor Webb calls for Brother Marcus to lead a song.

Through the excitement, I can hear the clanking sound from Sister Ophelia's metal walker. I close my eyes and pretend to pray.

You can't tell when she's sitting, but Sister Ophelia has severe scoliosis and walks completely bent forward at the waist.

"Sheela, go on and help Sister Ophelia to the bathroom" demands Grandmother in her sweetest voice. Her deep cocoa-colored hands push me to stand.

"Yes, Grandmother" I say, annoyed but unable to refuse.

Pointing my index finger in the air and shimmying over several knees towards Sister Ophelia, my thighs rub together loudly in my stockings. The elders look to acknowledge my raised finger before returning their attention to the pulpit.

"I got you" I whisper, confidently grasping Sister Ophelia's hand and pulling her onto her walker.

"Quit showing out!" I hear a deep voice whisper from across the room.

I'm flattered before seeing it's Christian, Sister Ophelia's grandson. He's like family and would probably be my husband if he could have waited for me.

He's standing by the sanctuary door, holding the communion plate in one hand and his crotch in the other.

"Gross. We're cousins" I mouth, looking at him with disgust and shaking my head.

"Play cousins." Christian responds silently, quickly

flicking his tongue before returning to the traditional usher's stance.

I hope everyone's view of his foolishness is blocked by Sister Ophelia's bent torso. He is what my grandmother calls mannish.

Our First Lady, Sister Webb, is leaving the bathroom as we approach. She corrects her slightly masculine gate as I greet her with a gentle smile and escort Sister Ophelia through the bathroom door. Sister Webb returns the gesture while checking the length of my skirt as I pass.

Pushing open the handicap stall door, I lift Sister Ophelia's dress and use the rail for support as I slowly lower her onto the modified toilet.

Her body vibrates as she abruptly releases the gas she's been holding during our walk through the sanctuary.

In shock, I allow her to fall onto the seat.

"Get on outta here, Baby. I'll holla when I'm ready." she says while adjusting her very large ass across the seat.

"Yes, ma'am." I respectfully convey before leaving the bathroom to stand outside the door.

The air is soft and the lights are dim in the sanctuary. Brother Marcus, our song leader, stands in his position at the front of the church. His tongue moves over his full chocolate lips as he sips water from a glass. He looks poised, delicious, and ready to direct us.

"Open your hymn books and turn to page 323. We're going to sing *There is a God*. Amen?" he begins while fingering the pages of the hymnal.

Brother Marcus's deep brown skin in his creamy yellow suit makes my mouth fill with water. I just want to stick my fork in that mac and cheese.

"If you have it, let the Church say Amen." prompts Brother Marcus as he looks out into the audience, starting the first note.

"Amen!" says the congregation.

"Amen!" repeats the voice in my head every time he licks his lips between measures.

Lick Amen! Lick Amen! Lick Amen!

As I think to myself, I feel heat rising between my legs.

"Sheela!" hollers Sister Ophelia from inside the bathroom, apparently frustrated.

"Yes, ma'am" I react quickly as I open the door.

I roll my eyes and take a deep breath. Irritated that she ruined my fantasy, but even more so by the smell of old urine and feces that now fills the air.

Taking quick breaths and without speaking, I help Sister Ophelia to the sink and out of the bathroom.

Thoroughly disgusted, I push her to walk a little more quickly. Arriving at her seat perturbed and slightly out of breath, I position Sister Ophelia comfortably at the end of our pew. As I sit down, a sigh of relief escapes my lungs when I cross my legs and flip through the pages of my hymn book.

My grandmother wears a large, feathered hat and sings in an operatic tone one octave above the harmony of the rest of the congregants. Because she's loud enough for the both of us, I sit here pretending to read along as she uses my thigh to pat out the rhythm. My tightened skin trembling below the undersized stockings she insists I wear.

Ending the notes in harmony with a sea of "Amen's" filling the air, the congregation stands, solemnly assessing their need to repent while silently judging the souls who walk towards the first row - sinner's row.

"Come on, Sheela." Grandmother says while forcefully pulling my arm.

"What? I haven't sinned. Stop pulling me, Grandmother, everyone's looking!"

I quietly express my displeasure while pushing my weight down into the seat.

"Come on, Sheela." my grandmother insists, now pushing me to leave our pew.

"Why Grandmother, what did I do?" I whine, questioning her as she continues to drag me with no explanation.

Arm-in-arm, Grandmother and I arrive at the altar. Christian stands there smiling while looking surprised.

"Do better, Sheela" he comments as he firmly hands me a repentance card.

My heart is pounding with anger and embarrassment.

I violently crumble my card in my hand, sick of Grandmother's theatrics and humiliation as I sit amongst the sinners on the first row.

I overhear Deacon Brigham speaking with concern to the sinner on my right.

"Now, look at me young lady, are you sure?"

Brother Brigham earnestly questions as he reads the comment section on her visitor's card.

Responding confidently, "Yes, sir, I've never been more sure."

She stands and removes the microphone from the Deacon's gripped hand.

"Good Morning. My name is Lela Mounds. I'm here visiting my grandfather, Brother Mounds."

Lela lifts her finger to gesture in the direction where Brother Mounds is sitting. There's a young couple with two children seated around him. They all stare intently at Lela, hanging on her every word.

"We all fall short of the Glory of God. Amen?" Lela continues, looking into the audience for confirmation.

"Amen" the congregation agrees in unison.

"Well...I've been in an intimate relationship with my sister's husband, Larry, for over seven years."

With this revelation, Lela looks sympathetically towards a couple in the back as a commotion stirs.

"Now that I've confessed and been forgiven by God, I can move forward in peace."

Lela finishes, covering her mouth as she sees her sister forcefully push through the sanctuary exit door with two small children in tow. Her husband, Larry, tries to keep up as he begs his wife to allow him to explain.

Sorrowfully dropping her head and holding the mic to her chest Lela states, "I hope for the sake of her soul that my sister can forgive me as God has."

"Okay, okay. Thank you, Sister Mounds. You might want to stay up here until after service." Deacon Brigham cautions Lela as he removes the microphone from her grasp.

"And lastly, Sister Diggs has a repentance to make. Please stand Sister Diggs."

Deacon Brigham offers me the microphone as he breathes a sigh of relief. I stand there, taking the microphone in protest. Mortified, I freeze, unable to face the disappointed masses as I continue to stare at him. He grips my padded shoulders, turning my body to face the crowd as I nearly faint, so pissed at my grandmother that I can barely breathe.

I'm tempted to regurgitate all the stories I've heard my grandmother gossip about but imagine being tackled before making it through one sentence.

Why am I here when this congregation is filled with old pimps and retired whores? If I wanted to, I could have already slept with several men at this church. Even the married, self-righteous ones that sit on the stage.

"Sister Diggs, do you have any repentance?" Deacon Brigham asks as if to hurry me, interrupting my trance.

"Excuse me? Why yes." I respond while clearing my throat.

"If I was going to end up sitting with the sinners, I should have just sinned! Life sounds way more interesting for them. I repent for trying to stick to the rules that obviously none of you are following!"

With this announcement, I quickly return the microphone to the Deacon and angrily walk back to my seat.

For the inconvenience, I purposely let my skirt hike up as I cross those in the pew before sitting down. I can't help that I have a big ass and I'm not about to apologize today.

Such hypocrites I scream in my head as I feel Grandmother return to the seat beside me. A furious heat radiates through her church coat.

"Everybody rise!" directs Brother Marcus as he approaches the podium for the closing song.

"Thank God!" slips from my lips as Grandmother pinches me, ripping a hole in my stockings.

"Girl, don't you use God's name in vain!"

Grandmother's piercing eyes express her threatening tone.

"Yes, Grandmother" I painfully respond.

I rub my hand over the hole in my stockings as I feel the broken skin on my thigh. The sting and blood cause me to hold my tongue, even though I believe she wanted to cause me harm on purpose.

I prepare to abandon my grandmother just as Brother Marcus sings *I want a mansion, robe and a crown*. His buttery smooth voice is easing the stinging pain from my wound. I'm healed just looking at those luscious chocolate lips. I bet his kisses are Hershey flavored.

Let me get them wet for you, Brother Marcus, I think to myself as the church noise quiets to a single tone. My imagination carries me deeper into erotic thoughts.

"Sheela!" quietly yells my grandmother, frowning while snatching my arm.

"Hurry and get to the Fellowship Hall before all the visitors start lining up. Make a plate for me, Sister Ophelia and your Aunt Khaki!"

"Yes, Grandmother. I'll get right on it."

I respond unenthusiastically as I collect my belongings.

"And don't put nothing on there that Sister Webb or Brother Jenkings made" she commands.

"I'm not playing, Girl. Last time I got sick as a dog!"

"Yes, Grandmother" I nonchalantly reply as I walk toward the Fellowship Hall's "Staff only" kitchen entrance.

The kitchen reminds me of my mother. She had the most eclectic set of cookbooks. She used to explain to me, "It's very important to season food according to the person you're serving."

He, Mr. Allen, burned most of her books when he set the house on fire. But I always hoped God saved one for me.

Walking into the kitchen, I see Sister Brigham hovering over an enormous pot, mashing spices, sugar and butter into a beautiful batch of steamed yams.

"Hey Baby! Are you doing okay?"

Sister Brigham sweetly turns to greet me, obviously referring to my humiliating outburst at the altar.

"I'm fine, Sister Brigham. Just stressed."

Looking at her innocently, she grips my hand.

"I know, Baby. It's hard not having a mother or a father to love on you, and your grandmother can be cold as ice, but she means well. Let Jesus be your rock" Sister Brigham expresses before placing a kiss on my forehead.

"You just need a plate for your grandmother, right?"

"Yes, ma'am. If you would please. And one for Sister Ophelia and my aunt Khaki as well. Oh, and please don't put anything on there that Sister Webb or Brother Jenkings made." I quickly add, relaying my grandmother's instructions.

"Alright, child! God damn it! You all are gonna have to pay me if you want a personal servant." Sister Brigham snaps while dumping the sweet yams into a glass serving bowl.

"Yes, ma'am."

I leave the kitchen rubbing the wound on my leg and briefly imagine telling Sister Brigham not to use God's name in vain. The thought of her unavoidable, hypocritical response brings joy to my soul.

Having already waited a while, I peak my head through the kitchen door as Sister Brigham points to three loaded plates covered in plastic wrap. I quickly hug her arm as she continues to work and place prepared plates onto a cart.

Walking into the crowded Fellowship Hall, I find my grandmother and Sister Ophelia sitting amongst the seniors.

"Is there anything else I can get for you, Grandmother? I need to get Aunt Khaki her food." I ask, handing them the overflowing plates.

Grandmother scoffs, "Get outta my face, Sheela, and you

better be in my house by 8:00 p.m. You hear me?"

"Yes, Grandmother." I reply before kissing her on the cheek and running through the exit doors.

Choosing Nurse Mitchell's school left me with a little extra money from my financial aid to finally buy my first car - a 1980 royal blue Monte Carlo. It's the only space I have to myself which I enjoy as I ride with the windows down and music up.

Approaching my Aunt's house, I hear a commotion. She says God closes his eyes on Sunday, so I'm sure she's drunk by now.

"Fuck you! You sorry mutha fucka!" Aunt Khaki yells from her front doorway while hurling a crumpled paper bag towards Uncle Ricky's Mercedes.

"You too, drunk bitch!" Uncle Ricky fires back, reversing his car from the driveway and taking off down the street.

Staring drunkenly at me as I park my car, Aunt Khaki uses her front doorway for support.

I jump out of my car, holding her plate in my hand as I walk toward her.

"Hey, Aunt Khaki. Is everything okay with Uncle Ricky?"

"Yeah Girl, I be fucking the shit out of Ricky. He'll be back!" Khaki laughs while lighting a joint and taking the plate from my outstretched hand.

"Did Sister Webb or Brother Jenkings make any of this shit?"

"No ma'am, I got you." I say, smiling while wafting the smoke from my face.

"Quit acting so damn innocent!"

Aunt Khaki laughs while pushing me playfully into the house.

Chapter 3

Stumbling over the coffee table, Aunt Khaki reveals the opened fifth of gin hidden under her leather sectional. Taking a sip, she begins to dance while moving her hands across her body. She doesn't acknowledge me as she continues to stumble through the house to her bedroom, collapsing face up onto her waterbed.

Watching this uneasy display, I ask, "You alright?" while walking into the room and rolling onto the bed.

"They think it's easy for pretty girls, but it's not."

Khaki's commentary sounds depressed as she stares at herself through the large mirror hanging overhead.

"Most men don't have the confidence to deal with us, so they steal our confidence instead."

"No man can steal my confidence." I declare as I move a little closer to my aunt.

"Shit! Girl, you're fucking crazy! There is no way God is going to let you be that pretty and be happy, too! Especially if you plan on being married!"

Khaki laughs so hard she falls from her bed.

"Looking on the bright side, at least this bottle of gin is half full."

Khaki leaves the bottle beside the bed and walks over to a tall, heavy mirror leaning against the corner. She strokes her body as she analyzes her reflection.

"You see, Sheela, God gave us a magical pussy, two big 'ol thighs and a behind to protect our hearts. Men can't fuck two things at once."

Aunt Khaki sounds confident while sucking her gold teeth and crossing her legs to sit on the ground. She grabs a pack of rolling papers before pulling a tray of crushed leaves onto her lap.

"It's crazy how being pretty works out. You spend your whole childhood pissed for being locked up like a porcelain doll, only to choose a man who'll do the same."

Khaki places the aromatic weed into the rolling paper before licking it close. Lighting the end, she takes a puff.

"You wanna hit this?" she offers.

I turn up my lips and shake my head in decline.

"You sure, girl? This is some good shit?"

The smell of marijuana smoke lingers in the air. I inhale the sweet, mellow aroma as I touch my thigh and consider my grandmother's punishment.

"What if she knows?" I timidly ask as I make eye contact with Aunt Khaki.

Shaking her head and retracting the lit joint, Khaki responds, "You're grown, Sheela."

"Ok, let me try." I say,

Hastily crawling to the floor to remove the joint from her fingers. Taking the first puff, I deeply inhale and then take another. The stress melts from my brain as I enjoy the sweet floral taste of the peppery herb. Returning the joint to my Aunt, I recline on the floor, consumed by magical thoughts and epiphanies.

After taking another toke, my aunt passes the joint back to me; I take another puff. Scooting to a box sitting beside her record player, Aunt Khaki fingers through the covers.

"*Prince*" Khaki reads from a record cover before setting the needle on the player. The sounds of hypnotic organ chords play through the speaker.

Aunt Khaki stands, positioning herself in front of the mirror.

Dearly Beloved... the song starts.

She winds her hips through her torso, lifting her hands in the air.

Let's go Crazy! she screams in unison with the voice on the record.

Dancing excitedly while pumping her fist in the air. Khaki pulls my limp body from the floor, forcing me to dance with her.

As we throw ourselves around the room in unison, I'm breathless, but too excited to stop. Pouncing together, we jump onto her waterbed and scream lyrics into the overhead mirror.

Fighting the violent waves of the water mattress, Aunt Khaki leaves the bed and walks into her closet. Out of breath, she takes off her clothes while dragging several garments behind her.

She jiggles her naked body in front of the mirror before pulling a shimmering red dress over her head. The deep neckline plunges to her belly and the split reveals her entire leg to the waist. Standing on her toes, she reminisces.

"I used to turn heads in this one. I'd walk into the club, take a seat at the bar, and have five men waiting to buy me a drink. Everybody in the club wanted this honey."

Khaki recalls as she devours her image and slowly removes the dress.

"Oh, and this one!"

Khaki laughs, picking a short, hot pink dress. She eagerly puts it on and struts around the room.

"This is the dress that bagged your Uncle Ricky. That bastard, I should throw this shit away." she announces before removing the dress and tossing it in the corner.

The needle on the player lifts and the next song begins. Spinning naked in the mirror, Khaki sings along,

I'm not a woman, I'm not a man, I am something that you'll never understand...

She gyrates her naked body toward the tray holding the awaiting joint and relights it. Coming to lie on the bed beside me, Khaki takes several puffs before passing it to me.

"My bad, I forgot you were a smoker now." she jokes.

I accept the now fingernail sized joint from her hand, place it to my lips and inhale the smoke.

"Ouch! I burned my lip." I scream, tossing the joint into the tray.

"Welcome to the club!"

Aunt Khaki turns her lip downward to reveal several burn marks on the inside.

"Try this one on!"

Aunt Khaki selects a white dress with golden embellishments.

"I want to see how it fits you."

Excited, my aunt begins removing my clothes. A feeling of euphoric relief travels through my body as she pulls the undersized stockings from my legs.

Standing naked with my aunt, I can't help but notice our family resemblance. Gathering the dress to make it easier for me to pull over my head, she steps back and places her hand over her mouth.

"Well?" I question, staring back at her.

"I'm fucking speechless. How come I didn't see it until now?"

Slowly approaching me and grabbing my shoulders, we turn to look in the mirror.

"My God, look at what your momma gave you." Khaki remarks, staring into my reflection.

"My momma had a body like this?"

I rub my hands over the dress as it hugs the curves of my body.

"Yep and I wouldn't show anybody if I was you. Hell, that's probably why Momma put you in those little ass church stockings!"

Khaki laughs hard while clapping her hands in the air.

"She saw that shit and was like hell no, not today!"

Shaking her head and walking towards the dresser, Khaki grabs a jar of cocoa butter and begins rubbing the cream on her hands.

"Didn't you bring my plate in here?" Khaki recalls, apparently feeling hunger pains.

"Oh yeah!"

I run excitedly out of the room. I have never been so happy to be reminded about a plate of food in my life. Apparently, marijuana makes me a different kind of hungry. A better kind. The thought of consuming the loaded plate of food warms my soul as I dance into the kitchen.

I return with the warm plate and place it on the side of the bed. We both kneel, and in silence, eat the mounds of soul food, savoring the enhanced flavor. Each delicious bite is followed by another until the plate is clean.

We fall back onto the floor with hands on our overly full bellies. Aunt Khaki's naked body lies sprawled on the carpet.

"Damn, that was good!"

Khaki rises to a sitting position while reaching for the tray of crushed leaves. I crawl over and rest my head on her thigh.

"Did my momma smoke?" I inquire as my aunt rolls the white paper around the leaves and uses her tongue to seal it close.

"No, but she made the best edibles. I remember her having a complete set of cookbooks dedicated to it. I'm still upset over losing that brownie recipe." she comments before bringing the joint to her lips to light it.

"See, Sheela, that's why you have to be careful. Some men will kill you before they see you with someone else."

Releasing the smoke from her lungs, she continues.

"Truth be told, I told your momma to stop that sexual healing bullshit long before that dude went crazy. Men are possessive over good pussy, whether they are already married or not. Shit! This pussy is magical. What's that leprechaun from the cereal box say?"

Khaki takes another puff and passes me the joint.

"It's magically delicious!" we say in unison, laughing onto the floor.

The sound of keys click in the lock.

"Fuck, what time is it?"

Aunt Khaki frantically reaches for her alarm clock.

"9:36. Fuck, Ricky's off work."

Aunt Khaki quickly lifts her body from the ground and assesses the messiness of the room.

"Put that out and help me throw all these dresses in the closet!" she mandates as she hands me a pile of clothes.

"Oh no! It's late! I have to go. Grandmother is going to kill me!"

I throw the dresses onto the closet floor and get my things prepared to leave.

"So, you're just going to sit here all day and smoke Uncle Ricky's weed, then leave me to deal with him? Family, them be the ones."

Khaki nervously pulls a mini skirt over her head.

"Really, Aunt Khaki?" I retort, looking at her still half naked body.

"Hey Uncle Ricky!"

I motion for a hug as he walks into the room.

"How're you doing, Sheela? Does your Grandmother know you're here smoking dope with my wife?" Ricky questions as he surveys the room and looks into my red, glossy eyes.

Uncle Ricky's attention moves to Aunt Khaki's naked legs as she stands there with her arms crossed, the mini skirt covering only her breast.

"Get on outta here, Sheela. I need to talk to my wife."

Uncle Ricky walks around me as he stares passionately at Aunt Khaki.

"I was just leaving."

I grab my shoes and purse as I rush to the front door.

Driving home, the stress returns to my brain and I allow fearful thoughts to flow through my mind.

The clock in my car says 10:12 as I arrive in front of my grandmother's house. The embellishments of my dress sparkle in the streetlights and my heels clack on the pavement as I step out of the car and walk up the steep drive to the house.

Approaching the door, I see Grandmother standing there, staring through the screen. Her furious eyes and small stature meet me on the porch as I approach the door.

"I know what it looks like, but that's not it at all."

The shock on her face gives me a glimpse into her thoughts.

"Look at you; a high-yella floozy, walking down the street with your arms, legs, and back all out! Get your big ass in this house before you catch a cold or a John."

"Yes Grandmother."

I take a deep breath as I try to enter the house, withholding my emotions before looking into her eyes.

"Do I sense an attitude, Sheela? What? Are you supposed to be grown now?"

Grandmother slams the screen door against the side of the house as she steps forward looking me dead in my eyes.

"No ma'am, I just lost track of time with Aunt Khaki and I'm really tired. Can I please come in now?"

As I walk towards the door, she pushes her hand against my shoulder to stop me.

"Yeah, you're tired alright. Just about as tired and sorry as your momma used to be. You might end up just like her the route you're going." she says, dropping her hand from my shoulder and looking me up and down.

"Yes Grandmother." I respond, hoping to end the verbal lashing.

As I move closer to the doorway, my grandmother yanks the side of my curly thick hair and brings it closer to her nose.

"Have you been smoking, Sheela? My God, you are such a disappointment.",

She shakes her head in disgust before releasing my hair.

"That's why you're so damn tired. You're out here on dope with your ass out! Then you want to walk in my house smelling like who did it and what for! You have lost your damn mind."

SEXMAGICFOOD

My grandmother grabs and jerks my arm before pushing
me into the house.

"Ouch! That hurts!", I scream as her nails dig into the
skin under my arm.

Slamming the door to the house, she releases my bruised
arm and walks towards the bathroom. I stand in the foyer,
realizing that I am now an unwelcome guest in my grandmother's home.

"Get in here!" she yells from the bathroom. I can hear the
shower running into the tub behind her.

"You think your dirty, dope fiend ass is about to walk
through my house?"

Her hand is extended from the bathroom door as I
approach.

"Take off that piece of trash you call a dress and get your
funky ass in this shower!"

Removing the dress, I stand naked in front of her. Feeling
much more ashamed of my body, I cover it with my hands as
I inch past her and get into the shower. Hoping she'll leave,
I quickly close the curtain, but she begins to talk through the
barrier.

"You know, Sheela, it seems that all I can make are pretty
girls with thick asses and small brains. I keep trying and ya'll
keep letting me down."

Grandmother takes a seat on the toilet and continues.

"I prayed to God after your Momma passed to please make
you easier on me than my girls were. Please don't let her be
a sex witch like her Momma or have her nose wide open like
her Aunt's. I've tried and tried, but I can hear destiny calling
your name. You're a whore Sheela. Just like your Momma.
I've been seeing it in you. That white man she got with to

27

make you left his mark too. You think too much, just like him."

Grandmother stops talking but groans a little as she pulls herself to stand.

"Well, classes are out tomorrow. You're going to clean this entire house from top to bottom, then go to Sister Webb's women's fellowship meeting. You hear me Girl?"

Placing a towel and night gown on the toilet seat, she removes herself from the bathroom.

"Yes, Grandmother. Thank you." I whimper, relieved as she closes the door.

Tears stream down my face and I drop to my feet. The water from the shower hits my body as I lay motionless in the tub, sobbing, breathless and exhausted.

My chest feels cold and empty, and the world goes silent. I pray, asking God to send me warmth, the love of my Momma and a glimpse of my Father. Urging Him to send it now so that I don't die here in the tub, but hoping that at least a part of me would.

More than an hour has passed, my skin is withered and I'm beginning to shiver. There is no warmth or love raining down as I had asked. Only chilly drips of water. Turning off the shower and reaching for the towel, I dry my body and slowly dress for bed.

Depressed, I stare into the mirror, further contemplating my loveless destiny before leaving the bathroom.

Tipping through the hall, I stop to see my grandmother sleeping peacefully in her room. The reflection of her black and white television bounces off the walls and her snore supersedes the noise from the program.

I walk in and stare at her for a moment, placing a kiss on her cheek and whispering, "Maybe you're right Grandmother.

I guess we'll see."

I pull the blanket to cover her shoulders before continuing to my bed.

There's something calming about walking into my cold bedroom at the end of the day. The ceiling fan moves the smell of scented vanilla candles through the air, and my mood is mellowed by the warm soft glow of the nightlight. I climb on top of my heavily pillowed bed, placing the yellow decor on my reading chair before sliding between the fresh cotton sheets. The comforter is heavy on my body as I relax into the dense softness, allowing today's events to flash through my mind.

Sexual healing? Sex witch? The new revelations on my Momma's life consume my thoughts as I grow depressed, desperate to know more.

The coldness in my chest intensifies as hot tears run down my face into the pillow. I imagine what life would be like if I had my Momma.

She would know just what to say, I think to myself, wishing for an answer. Maybe being a whore won't be so bad. It's got to be better than this, I envision, attempting to lift my spirit.

I flip my pillow to the cooler side and wedge another pillow between my legs. Dark thoughts and erotic visions creep from my mind, leaking into my cold empty chest and filling the space once reserved for love. My body loses consciousness, winning the fight as the torture of my mind ceases, allowing me to sleep peacefully until the morning.

Chapter 4

"Hurry up, Renada! You're going to get us caught!"

"I'm trying Christian, but this grass is still wet and bugs keep hopping on me!"

"Be quiet!" says Christian, pulling his sister, Renada to the back of the house.

Christian tosses small rocks at my windows while loudly whispering my name.

Groggy and disoriented, I rise from my bed, open the window and drop a small fire escape ladder down to them. They both crawl in through the opening, bringing wet grass in on their feet.

"Not cool! Y'all getting dirt all on my floor!" I say, grabbing a towel from my laundry bin and gesturing for them to wipe their shoes.

"What's up? Why are y'all crawling through my window at 5:00 in the morning?"

I'm exhausted and my eyes are heavy from the night before.

"Hold up! Wait, so you don't know you're the talk of the granny hotline?" says Renada, looking confused and bucking her eyes at me.

"Your grandmother is telling everybody that you were out in the streets last night with your ass out smoking dope! Lord, I just can't lose my best friend to the streets! God, please help her!"

Renada cries and paces in circles while shaking her hands

in the air.

"Chill, Renada! I got this." says Christian in a cool tone while walking towards me. His expression is serious as he softly grabs my hands.

"Sheela, all I'm saying is that you're wrong for not letting me hit that pussy first! Fake cousin bullshit to the side, I've been trying for years and all this time you've been whoring around! You're wrong, Sheela, dead wrong! And you owe me, you owe me a lot."

Christian dramatically releases my hands and looks me up and down. He takes a moment to stare at my thighs before turning and placing his hands on his head.

"First of all, y'all need to calm down!" I say, feeling slightly violated as I take a deep breath and begin to explain.

"I was wearing my Aunt's party dress because I lost track of time and ran from her house with it on. I wasn't in the street whoring around like my Grandmother is gossiping about. Second, I wasn't smoking dope! Well, I take that back. I smoked two joints with my Aunt." I confess, hiding my face and pausing for their response.

"So, wait. You smoked weed for the first time without me?" asks Renada, disheartened that our long-standing promise had been broken.

"Alright, Sheela, check this out. We can forgive you, if you brought some weed back to share with us. Did you think enough of us to do that?" inquires Christian, standing over me as I sit on my bed.

"No." I say,

My voice softened with hesitation.

"Really? Sheela! You're just dragging us through the mud at this point!", says Christian, as he and Renada argue back and forth in disappointment.

Renada shames Christian for cheating on me in high school, breaking my heart and making me run to the streets. Christian declares Renada a terrible friend for not realizing I was a whore sooner.

"Y'all just sit down a second so I can tell you everything."

I pull both of their arms to sit on the bed as I stand to explain.

I emotionally re-enact each moment of my grandmother's cruelty as they watch me from the bed.

I finish and we all sit quietly for a moment, considering the events I just relayed to them in confidence.

Christian laughs and breaks the silence.

"Dang! Your Grandmother went off on you.

"Well, I guess that makes me feel a little better. Good job Grandma.", he says, looking away while smiling to himself.

Annoyed, I turn my attention to Renada.

"I'm sorry Sheela. Don't believe your Grandmother! She's just a mean old biddy."

Renada leans over to grab my face and put her forehead to mine.

"Back up Renada!" says Christian, standing and pulling her from my bed.

"Let's go before Sheela's grandmother wakes up. God knows she deserves her rest." says Christian, sarcastically, as he walks towards the window with his sister.

"You guys are a mess! See you at service." I say, helping them out of the window before closing it shut.

I watch from the window as they run through the grass to the neighboring abandoned lot. My heart sinks as they disappear from my view and I feel dishonest. Although I had spent all that time explaining, I conveniently left out the part where I decided that being a whore wouldn't be so bad. I mean, if my Momma put it in me, how could it be bad.

Besides, I don't feel like hearing Renada talk about the sacredness of my body and I don't want to hear Christian argue about why he should be my first.

My grandmother probably scared off my future husband anyway. Why does she have to be such a gossip? It's crazy how she can tell everyone about my business but won't tell me anything about herself.

I'm all she's going to talk about on her women's trip.

I can hear her saying, Sheela had on a rag for a dress... Sheela came into my house smelling like a dope fiend.

She'll be the highlight of the trip and everyone will pray for her. Everything is always about her.

"Sheela!" Grandmother calls to me from the bathroom.

"Yes Grandmother!" I respond from my room.

There are a few moments with no response before I call out again,

"Yes Grandmother!" I say, just a little louder.

Putting on my robe and slippers, I leave my room and walk towards the open bathroom door. She's sitting naked on the side of the tub, bathing herself with soap and running water.

"Good Morning, Grandmother.", I say as I arrive at the bathroom door.

"Hand me that towel over there on the sink." she requests, turning off the water.

I hand the towel to her and adjust the flickering gas furnace on the wall.

"Is there anything else, Grandmother?"

"Just make a little breakfast before I go. The bus is going

to pick me up in an hour." she says quickly, hurrying me to get started.

"Yes, Grandmother."

I head towards the kitchen, reciting a recipe to myself.

"A pinch of salt and a little sugar, 1 cup of flour, 1 egg, and 1 cup of milk."

Grabbing a bowl from the shelf, I mix the ingredients and ladle the smooth mixture into a hot buttered pan. Searing each side to a golden brown, one after another, I pile the fluffy hotcakes onto a plate. I slice slabs of butter to melt between their layers and drizzle warm maple syrup over the top as the last touch.

"Here's your breakfast, Grandmother."

I happily place the plate on her TV tray and arrange her cutlery.

"Thanks, Sheela. Don't forget to get the house cleaned up today while I'm gone. I mean top to bottom!" she reminds me before slicing into the stacks of hot buttery cakes.

"Yes Grandmother."

I smile gently in her direction before turning to walk away.

Alone in the kitchen, I enjoy a small plate for myself. There's only two misshapen pancakes made from the final bits of batter, but the crispy edges and extra maple syrup make every bite into a delicacy.

I hear heavy metal brakes squealing outside the house. The church bus driver signals his arrival with a quick tap on the horn.

"Grandmother, the bus is here!" I yell as I jump from my seat, trying not to sound too excited.

I walk into her room and remove the plate and utensils from her TV tray before helping her to her feet.

"Do you need my help with anything else?" I ask, quickly grabbing her small overnight bag from the floor and looking around the room.

"Yes, I need your help getting out of my way! I declare! This child is trying to toss me out the front door." she pronounces while laughing to herself as I slide her purse onto her shoulder.

"Well, I think that's everything Grandmother. You don't want to keep the bus waiting. I'll take care of the house and see you when you get back." I say, kissing her cheek and encouraging her out onto the porch.

"Well, alright. And don't forget about Sister Webb's women's meeting tonight.", she mentions again as I help her down the steps and onto the steep lawn.

"Yes, Grandmother."

Walking arm-in-arm with her, we stop in front of the bus.

She climbs the steps, using the railing to push through the entry and slowly meanders down the center aisle, cackling with the other seniors as she finds her seat. I lift my hand and salute the bus driver as he pulls away. The bus brake light flashes red as it makes the corner, disappearing from my view.

I stand outside enjoying each second of her departure before heading back inside of the house.

Closing and locking the front door, I dance into my room and rush for the radio. The speakers tremble as I crank up the loaded snare and techno beats.

My girl wants to party all the time... sings the voice on the blasting radio as I dance into a sweat and strip from my clothes. My body feels lighter as I move naked through my room.

The bounce of my reflection catches my attention and I

stop naked in front of my mirror, feeling sexy and considering my body. I hold my breast with my palm and lift them while standing on my toes.

The contours of my waist lead to a triangle shaped gap between my thighs.

The bottom curve of my ass shows through to the front and I admire the view.

My brown nipples slip through my open fingers.

Sexily adoring my body while posing in the mirror, my hands slowly glide across the soft peaks and deep valleys. Each sensual observation takes me deeper into my imagination and my temperature rises.

"Come over here and lick this. I'm thick and sweet like honey, so you might get a little sticky." I say, fantasizing and feeling myself. Licking my lips as I prepare for bliss.

I move my hand between my legs, part the lips, and slip my fingers inside. A sharp, warm pleasure carries itself through my body as I stroke my fingers firmly up, down, and in circles.

Moaning and grabbing my breast, I slide my fingers down and insert them deep inside, curling them forward and pulsing in and out as I imagine being penetrated and pleasured.

Moaning louder, tingles shoot up and down my spine.

Wetness drips down my fingers as I continue to stroke myself, tilting my head back as the euphoric feeling fuels my fantasies.

"Your lips are so soft...kiss it right there." I whimper to myself. Gently circling my fingers around as my legs weaken.

My body convulses as the euphoria climaxes between my legs. Breathing heavily, electricity slowly moves through my lips and into the space around me.

Returning to my heavily pillowed bed, I set my alarm

and slide between the sheets. Relaxed and satisfied, I cup my hand between my legs and allow the weight of my comforter to lull me back to sleep.

Chapter 5

Forcing my thick, tangled hair into a top bun, I slide into an oversized cotton T-shirt before starting my chores.

Piles of superfluous household items cover the floor as I organize and purge my grandmother's hoard.

Thirty bath towels and over eighty unopened bars of soap start the Goodwill pile as the mass of unused toiletries grows even more daunting.

I toss buckets of partially melted soap and curiously labeled medicine bottles into the trash from the cabinets below the sink. Several wigs lay abandoned, along with an innumerable collection of empty product containers.

Dust particles fill the air as I forcefully disturb each corner of the hidden spaces.

Hours pass and the air feels fresher as each completed room is marked by a lit candle.

My grandmother's bedroom door is propped open by several handbags as I begin the final task of straightening her room.

"Why does she have so much shit!" I inquire, screaming out loud after several hours of silence, exhausted and discouraged by the newly revealed stash.

"I mean, this is ridiculous! She's over here knee deep in bullshit and she calls me lazy! I declare!" I yell out emotionally drained while carelessly sweeping accumulated trinkets from her shelves.

What's that?, I wonder to myself as a leather-bound

book falls onto the ground. It looks handmade and is heavily engraved.

Stepping over the various obstacles scattered in front of the closet door, I grasp the book by its sturdy binding and flip it open. There is a beautifully handwritten inscription across the first page.

I dedicate this book to my Love Vinny and his wife, Jane Marie. A man who shares his bed with a frigid woman often finds healing in my sweet waters.

Closing the book, I spin it between my hands while running the tips of my fingers across the engraved lettering.

Sex Magic and Food: Cannabis Enchantments, is on the cover. *Volume 6* is on the spine.

A scream of excitement escapes my lungs and I leap onto my grandmother's bed to obsess over the pages.

The book cover is worn and heavily tattered at the corners, but the print and color illustrations are perfectly preserved. The pages are slightly yellow and dank, but the quality of the paper is sturdy between my fingers.

A curvy woman with full breast and hips is stretched in various sexual positions throughout the pages. Her face is painted with an expression of ecstasy.

Submissive does not mean weak. Clasping your hands behind your back confirms your gentleman fills you with joy and commitment to serve..." I read from a note below the illustration.

Tears fall from my eyes as I thank God, realizing I finally

hold a piece of my Momma. Time stops as I sniff the pages, growing closer to her ghost and feeling a warmth come over me I've never felt before.

I continue to read randomly from the pages, diving back into the trove of sexual treasure. My mind is swimming with new information as I try to rationalize the reasoning.

Sexless marriages cause loneliness, and loneliness leads to death. When divorce is not an acceptable option, honest men receive sexual pleasure outside of their marriage in order to stay married. The ritual healers who serve these men are called Daughters of Sweet Water..." As I read aloud, I'm startled by the ringing of the telephone.

Time starts again as I jump over several piles.

Running to the kitchen, I catch the call.

"Hello, This is the Diggs residence. How can I help you?" I say to the caller, waiting for a response.

"Sheela! This is your grandmother. What's going on over there?" she demands, stopping to hear my list of accomplishments.

"I'm almost done, Grandmother. I'm working on your room now. Did you know you had over eighty unused bars of soap in the hall closet?" I ask, wondering if she'd intentionally accumulated the cache.

"Just get it done, Sheela! And don't forget about Sister Webb's Women's Fellowship tonight. You've got a couple of hours to get clean and get there!" she commands.

"Yes, ma'am. I love you." I respond as the phone disconnects in my ear.

Climbing back through the piles, I place the book carefully on the dresser and continue to sort my grandmother's hoard.

The words from the pages and the elegance of my

Momma's writing echoes between my ears. I'm eager to return to my studies and fall deeper into my Momma's footsteps.

Minutes turn into hours and my grandmother's floor is rendered bare. I mark her room as complete with a lit candle before grabbing my newly prized possession and heading to my room.

Sliding the book below my mattress for safekeeping, I remove my now heavily soiled clothes and sprint naked to the shower.

Sister Webb's meeting starts in thirty minutes and I feel quite dirty.

Chapter 6

My right breast threatens to pop from my silk blouse as I run through the sanctuary.

I open the door of the meeting room while fixing my stressed buttons and almost run into Sister Brigham. She's holding a clipboard and greets me with a pleased look as I walk through the door.

"Well, Hello Sister Diggs! I'm blessed to see you here tonight. Come on and sign in." she says while handing me the clipboard.

"Yes ma'am, I'm blessed to be here. I look forward to learning from my Sisters." I reply, politely returning the clipboard and heading towards the circle of women.

Most of the Sisters stare as if I should be in Children's Church as I take my seat. Everyone is talking amongst themselves and I can't help but to think some of the comments are about me.

The Singles Ministry fell apart a couple of months ago when a mega-church opened down the street. I was forbidden to go there by my grandmother, so this meeting is my only option.

I consider leaving, feeling nervous as Sister Webb stares at me from across the room. She's not wearing any makeup and her chemically straightened hair is pulled back into a tight bun. She crosses her leg at the knee, and she seems to look through me as I fidget with my Bible.

"Welcome to our fellowship Sister Diggs!" yells Sister

Webb over the cacophony of conversations, smiling and waving her hand.

"Thank you, Sister." I respond, returning a gracious smile and nodding my head.

"Good evening everybody! Welcome to the Women of God in Christ Fellowship meeting." Sister Webb says loudly, standing from her seat as the Sisters quiet their individual conversations.

"Last week we talked about sexual relations in Christian marriages and couldn't seem to get to a stopping point. Let's pick up where we left off."

Sister Webb briefly shifts her eyes to notes before looking up at me.

"Oh, and Sheela, I know you're the only one left from the Singles Ministry so you can just listen and ask questions if you feel the need, okay? Let's hear from Sister Jenkings first."

Sister Webb grabs her ink pen and turns towards a thin-framed, light-complected woman on her left.

Sister Jenkings adjusts the cuffed sleeves of her blouse before taking a deep breath and looking at the faces around the room.

"Good evening Sisters. I can't believe I'm saying this, but I haven't made love to my husband in two years. I never intended for it to get this bad, but I don't know what to do. It's like he's lost interest in me." Sister Jenkings drops her head with this confession.

"Please continue Sister Jenkings." says Sister Webb, urging her gently while placing an arm around her shoulder.

"Well, I know that a man has needs and all, but I'm not the woman who will let him do his business on me whenever he feels like it. I need to be in the mood before he goes rubbing and kissing on me. He was persistent at first, but I must have pushed him away one too many times. It's like he doesn't see me now.

I don't like the fact that he's changing completely just because were not having sex. I should mean more to him than that. I'm his wife!" says Sister Jenkings as she begins to sob.

"I don't want to be married to a man who only sees me as a sex toy.",

Clutching her skirt, she cries as she ends her testimony.

I'm silent as the Sisters around the circle speak up in support. It seems they all believe Brother Jenkings should be more understanding, maybe try a little harder before giving up. They encourage her to stand firm until he breaks, acknowledging that a man can only go so long without sexual pleasure from his wife.

"But don't stop cooking though!" says an elderly Sister, interjecting from the circle.

"Your man has to eat somewhere, don't give him any excuses."

Laughter and confirmation spring from the group as Sister Webb raises her hand, grabbing everyone's attention.

"Now ladies, sexual intercourse with your husband is part of being a good wife. God knows I understand you feel used, especially when you'd rather have things another way, but you have to make love to your husbands. That's acceptable and pleasing in God's eyes." she says, firmly placing her hand over Sister Jenkings knee and giving her an understanding smile before returning to her list.

"Sister Marcus, you and Brother Marcus have been married for about eight years now, right?" Sister Webb asks as she looks towards a sharply-dressed woman sitting across from her in the circle.

"Um, yes. Just made it eight years." she replies, nodding

her head in Sister Webb's direction.

"Congratulations Sister, would you like to share testimony or lean on the group for support?"

The chairs creek and grind against the linoleum floor as the Sisters adjust their position to face Sister Marcus. The room is silent with anticipation as she speaks.

"Good evening Sisters. Brother Marcus and I have been married for eight years", She says, reminding everyone as she quickly lifts her heavily jeweled finger to push her hair behind her ear.

"We're still in love, but he's gotten to where he wants to explore new things, sexual positions and even fellatio. I love my husband, so sex once a month is not a problem, but putting his penis in my mouth is not required for him to, you know, finish."

Sister Marcus, looks around the room as everyone stares quietly in her direction.

"He asks me to get more freaky and loosen up; to stop giving so many directions, but sex is supposed to be for two people. He's already feeling good as soon as he starts, I need him to do exactly what I say so I can feel good too." she explains after standing slightly to pull down her leather skirt and return to her seat.

"I'm just not that type of woman. My Momma didn't raise me to bow down under a man's genitalia, husband or not!" says Sister Marcus, passionately finishing her testimony and awaiting response from the gallery.

I dare not respond as the Sisters cheer her on in support.

Sister Webb continues down the list as each Sister recalls a taboo sexual request offered by their husbands. They speak softly and explain the torrid details hoping God is not listening in judgement. Their hands move through the air describing sexual penetration points before quickly being hidden away.

"So, I looked him straight in the eye and said, No sir, that is called sodomy." a short, stout Sister passionately expresses before sitting back in her seat.

As the conversation continues, Sister Webb and the Elders encourage us to abstain from participating in explicit sexual acts. They decree that men are ruled by the flesh and should not be judged on their urges but be refused on all occurrences. Women of God cannot submit to the ways of men. Those who submit to the ways of the flesh are nothing but common whores.

Although the dense gravity of the caucus was meant to deter me from entertaining the sexual fantasies in my head, it only turned me on.

I imagine stretching my body across the bed as their husbands take their frustrations out on me. Gripping and turning my body, penetrating me forcefully and moaning in ecstasy.

Brother Marcus can put his penis in my mouth. I'll get on my knees and let him teach me how he likes it.

"Sheela!" Sister Webb shouts as if it were the fifth time.

"I'm sorry, I got lost in my thoughts." I say, snapping out of my trance.

"Do you have questions?" she asks, chuckling at my dazed expression.

"No ma'am. Thank you! I've learned a lot."

I smile and look around at the Sisters in the circle.

"That's a blessing.", Sister Webb responds before asking everyone to bow their heads for closing prayer.

Afterwards, they all cluster to chat as no one is in a rush to leave.

An elderly Sister lectures Sister Jenkings by the snack table. Encouraging her to reconsider the dissolution of her marriage and to get a little more meat on her bones.

Sister Webb and Sister Marcus remain seated, entranced by each other as they continue to speak about the firm boundaries within marital relationships. Light reflects from the rocks on their ring fingers as hand gestures explain how far they are unwilling to go.

There are corners of silent prayer and secrets being swapped between Sisters. My age and lack of marital commitment makes me an unnecessary bystander.

Placing my purse on my shoulder and walking towards the door, I see no one pay attention as I wave my hand goodbye.

"Are you a virgin Sheela?" I hear a voice question from my right.

Turning, I see Sister Brigham. Her hands are full of collected paper cups and crumpled napkins. She looks at me as if it's a question she had been pondering for a while.

"Yes ma'am." I uncomfortably answer, while glancing around the suddenly hushed room.

"That's a blessing." she replies as she continues to collect trash from the circle.

"Your Sisters are here for you. Let us know when you've got your eye on someone special." she says, winking her eye at me as all the Sisters stare in my direction.

"Of course. You all have a blessed night." I say, walking through the doorway to leave as quickly as possible.

"You think she's one of those lesbians everybody's trying to be now?" I hear an older lady whisper before quickly being hushed by Sister Webb.

Chapter 7

My car glides on the road as I unconsciously drive home, high on erotic thoughts, consumed by a desire for sexual intercourse.

Somehow arriving home, my hand guides the key into the lock, and pushes open the front door.

Retiring to my room, I sit comfortably in my reading chair with the soft light of my floor lamp glowing above my head. My momma's book is laid across my folded legs, pressed open on the first page.

My body is still, and I dedicate my mind to the offerings of each carefully written note. My fingers glide along the page as I read.

> *Daughters of Sweet Water, healing should be kept in secret. Pleasure and be pleasured in the dark shadows where judgment does not live. Submit to the uncelebrated ecstasy that is your life. Choose your gentlemen very carefully and never stray from the rules.*

I read, stopping a moment to digest.

Turning the page, a delicate garland of bright yellow roses, dripping with golden honey, is painted around the perimeter of a framed list. I feel the grooves of the lettering with my fingertips before continuing to read a numbered list of rules.

> *WARNING: The rituals in this volume create an intense love cycle that must be honored every 28*

days. All bonds created must be handled with care.

1. *Must not be practiced by an inexperienced virgin*
2. *Only bond with the married.*
3. *Do not stray from the recipe.*
4. *Create the bond: Place semen from yoni into a yellow candle. Light it.*
5. *Impede the bond: Speak "Our bond for now is broken. Tonight was only nice. Return this love to your wife." thrice over the flame.*

The list ends and I read it again. I'd already be breaking the first rule if I use this magic. The warning also gives me pause.

Guilt consumes me as I consider the heaviness of this sin, but I can't fight the temptation to continue.

Turning the page, a description of the first ritual immediately starts.

Session One: Wall Submission

A depiction is drawn of a full-figured naked woman with her hands gripping the wall as she stands on her toes, bent at the waist.

Looking below the art, I read a recipe for Chocolate Covered Strawberries.

Crouch over the bowl or insert your fingers into your yoni and use them to stir the chocolate before adding the cannabis butter ..."

I read from the instructions, becoming nervous and looking back at the depiction.

*Make nine strawberries and feed the gentleman
from your hand before submitting against the wall.
Once he has finished, immediately and discreetly
collect the semen into the yellow candle for conse-
cration. The candle must be lit before escorting the
gentleman to the door in order to release the love
energy. Saving distressed marriages is the purpose
served by the Daughters of Sweet Water. We are the
servants of love."*

I read from the ending lines of the page before closing
the book.

I deeply exhale, unconscious of the fact that I had stopped
breathing.

Frightened and apprehensive, I question my ability to
be a Daughter of Sweet Water. I'm no longer sure I have the
confidence my momma possessed.

Nothing about this feels right, but nothing feels wrong
either.

These men are suffering, but what about the wives, my
sisters? I would never want to hurt them, but their marriages
are in danger.

God has placed me in the position to know their pain and
given me the desire to help. I don't want to take anything from
them, only add relief.

I stare at the list of rules and my stomach grows nauseous.

I'm ready to be a Daughter of Sweet Water like Momma,
but I'm unsure about what that means for my soul.

My arms cross to hold the book to my chest before sliding
it between the layers of my mattress.

The quiet is loud and I'm too consumed to move, before

hearing a knock on the door. Checking my clock, I notice the late hour before walking from my room.

"Who's there?" I ask, suspiciously looking at a shadowy figure through the peephole.

"It's me, Renada! I forgot to return your anatomy book.

My psychological load lifts as I quickly unlock and open the door. Renada's teased curls mash against my face as I embrace her, squeezing her tightly around her neck.

Everything I want to tell her races through my mind as I continue to hold her. Not wanting her to see my eyes.

"What happened?", she manages to say with her voice muffled by my armpit.

"I'm just tired of trying to please everyone. I just want to be myself. But who would love me if I did that?"

Sounding dejected, I release her from my embrace.

"You'll always have me, Sheela. No matter what."Renada says trying to give me reassurance, but looking concerned.

"Is this about nursing school? I know it's stressful, but we're almost done. Plus, Nurse Mitchell said we can have a key to the simulation room so we can get ahead."

Renada reaches into her bejeweled purse before handing me a freshly made silver key and gripping my hand.

"But anyway, be who you want to be, Sheela. How will we ever know who we are until we try to find out?"

Shrugging her shoulders and releasing my hand, Renada turns back towards the door.

"Gotta run! Oh, and don't forget about the church picnic on Friday. Christian will drop me off so we can ride together. Love you!", says Renada, closing the door behind her.

Stripping from my clothes, I darken my room and slide between the layers of my cotton sheets. Cozy under the heavy down of my comforter, in my cold, vanilla scented room, I lie awake. Praying to my momma for a sign.

Chapter 8

Ten women and three men sit across six steel tables with textbooks open, looking toward the front of the classroom. All of their eyes rest on Nurse Mitchell's thin lips and stern face as she calls names from the roll book.

"Sheela Diggs."says Nurse Mitchell, surveying each seat for my face.

Renada gestures to communicate her unawareness as Nurse Mitchell stares in her direction.

Zealously removing a pen from her pocket, Nurse Mitchell places a red mark beside my name and continues the lecture.

I know my class is disappointed as I lay comfortably in my room, spending extra time reading from Momma's book.

> *"Does the seed want to be buried and cracked open from within, and does the rose want to be cut at the stem from its roots? The answer to these questions is, yes, of course.*
>
> *The unopened seed rots and the unchosen rose dies without being treasured for its beauty.*
>
> *Dear Daughter, crack open your seed and be chosen. Only you decide how your story ends."*

I can almost hear her voice as I read.

I thank God that I'll never live in a world without my momma's words again before sliding the precious book between the layers of my mattress.

Climbing from bed, I look through my wardrobe and disgust overtakes me, intruding on the space I had left for my

Grandmother's opinion.

"These are old lady clothes.", I say to myself, pushing through the rows of wire hangers in my closet.

Thick ankle-length skirts, long sleeve blouses and boutique dresses repeat in different tones and fabrics.

I've got to get some clothes that are a little more me. I declare as I reach for my keys and close the closet door.

Just as I start my car, I remember that I'm supposed to wait for Renada, but continue to drive, determined to find a fresh new look.

Loud pop music plays through the speakers of the colorful boutique. The saleswoman is holding a lilac purple skirt set, showing me the detailed pleats on the cheerleader style skirt and the perfectly placed bow on the back of the shirt. Promising it will enhance my figure.

"You'll look great! Guys will stop you on the street!" she says while placing the set over my arm and rushing me to the dressing room.

I allow the dressing room mirror to exaggerate the flaws in my thin oversized underwear before removing the skirt from the hanger and pulling it over my body.

The zip is perfect, and the fabric sways softly as I shift in the mirror. The expertly stitched top slides effortlessly over my ample breasts, comfortably cinching my waist and snapping to a close.

Revealing myself from the dressing room to the exterior mirror, the saleswoman screeches.

"Your bod is hella rad in that outfit! You must take it!" she insists as I spin in the mirror causing my skirt to lift and expose my thighs.

"Ring it up!" I say enthusiastically as I hand her the tags.

I place my old clothes in the shopping bag and smile as the door chimes when I leave the shop.

Excited, I drive to the church picnic, arriving at a record speed as I park my car and check myself in the mirror.

Stepping onto the parking lot, my courage fades and I regret my decision not to wear jeans as the long pleats of my skirt lift in the wind, forcing me to return to my car for protection against the violent gusts.

Checking my surroundings, I notice the church tent canopies threatening to blow onto the lawn as the Brothers work together to anchor their poles to the ground.

I can see my grandmother standing at the curb of the lot. Shading her eyes before walking in my direction.

A black net holds her long gray hair in place as she fights the wind to reach me. Her short thick legs rub slightly as she walks, slowing her down just enough to cause frustration.

"Sheela! Get yo tail out of the car and help Sister Brigham set up this dessert table!" Grandmother yells while gripping the handle of my car door and pulling it open.

A dramatic gasp and wide eyes grace her expression as she reaches towards the hem of my skirt.

"What in the tarnation do you have on?" Grandmother howls, grasping my skirt before dropping the gentle fabric onto my lap.

"It's a skirt set. It's different, but I think it looks nice on me." I respond, testing my ability to remain confident.

"Ain't nothing nice about how you look in that Sheela. Get over to my car and look through that Goodwill bag. It's probably something better in there than what you have on."

My attention is drawn to her sky blue Cutlass parked nearly unseen behind the Fellowship Hall.

"Yes Grandmother."

I exhale and roll my eyes with complete exhaustion of her continued meddling.

I brace my arms to my side, holding my skirt taught as I quickly gallop towards the rear of Grandmother's car.

A shadow leaps from the side of the Fellowship Hall, frightening me, before inviting me into a secret conversation.

"So, you mean I'm supposed to go without sex for two years and just be good with you! You're out of your goddamn mind!" I hear Brother Jenkings yelling at someone angrily in a hushed voice.

"Do you think I'm not a man just because I'm a Christian? You're my wife and I love you, but I have needs! This denial is killing me. It's been killing me. Our marriage can't survive like this", he declares in almost a whisper.

I hear gravel kick under his feet before a female voice climbs from the shadows.

"Well, I'm just disappointed. I thought you loved me for my heart and God-fearing spirit, not the hole between my legs. I want to be with you for the rest of my life, but I just feel strange knowing that sex is the only way you'll stay with me. Yes, sex is important to a marriage, but we need to get our relationship together before we hump around in bed."

Her voice stops, but I recognize it as Sister Jenkings.

The wind threatens to toss me into their view before Brother Jenkings responds to his wife. There is a pain in his voice as he urges her to understand.

"Baby, I love you, you know I do, but I don't know what to do with this." he admits softly.

I hear his feet shuffle toward her as she speaks.

"Well, you know what you can do, find somebody else

to handle all that, I'm not trying to be your sex toy, I'm your wife!" Sister Jenkings asserts, rushing away from him, exposing my position at the corner.

We bump into each other and exchange apologies before I can continue to my grandmother's car.

I see Brother Jenkings leaning against the side of the building with one foot propped up for support. He's aggressively smoking a cigarette and speaking in frustration to himself. I catch his eye and he continues to watch me walk to my grandmother's car.

"Hey Brother Jenkings!" I yell out to him from across the lot.

"You look nice, Sheela." he replies, softly running his manicured fingers across his smooth jawline.

"Why thank you, sir!" I express as I look innocently in his direction.

The bend of his knee leads my eyes to the crotch of his perfectly tailored pants. I briefly molest his bulge with my eyes before looking away.

I can feel his eyes continuing to watch me as I carefully consider how to release my skirt and open the trunk.

I glance over my shoulder as he takes another pull from his cigarette and continues his stare. I fight the temptation to look again, pretending not to notice.

I can hear the jingle of Brother Jenkings keys as he shifts his position against the wall. He's still watching as I push my skirt between my legs, attempting to hold it in place as I crouch down slightly to open the trunk of my grandmother's car.

The wind calms for a moment, fueling my courage as I release both of my hands from my skirt, using them to loosen the tightly pulled knots in the clothing bags.

I feel comfortable for several moments before a violent gust of wind lifts my skirt. Exposing my thin, oversized underwear and full thighs to Brother Jenkings now lustful eyes.

Gasping and scrambling to put my skirt back in place, I leap into the trunk of my grandmother's Cutlass and quickly turn to make eye contact with Brother Jenkings.

Unwavering, he lifts his cigarette, takes a pull and continues his stare. Gently licking his lips before displaying a charming grin.

My heart rate quickens, and my panties moisten. Looking away, I remove a pair of bleach burned jeans from the Goodwill bag and return my eyes back to his.

Watching him take another pull from his cigarette, I stare at him as I unzip my skirt and recline against the clothing bags. Slowly slipping my skirt down over my knees, I open my legs wider towards him. The moist sheer fabric of my underwear hiding nothing from his view.

"Damn Sheela." I watch him mouth from across the lot while stepping forward, glancing left and right to check our surroundings.

I laugh, climbing from the trunk and hurrying to hide from view to struggle into the undersized jeans. Turning around, jumping and twisting, I force the material over my ass onto my waist. I'm out of breath as I fasten the jeans, not noticing he's left his position on the wall.

I hear gravel kicking across the lot as he hurries in my direction. My heart pounds, rendering me speechless, as I search for something magical to say.

"You really shouldn't play with grown men like that little girl." Brother Jenkings admonishes as I make eye contact with him and walk away.

"Sheela, wait. Why are you walking off like that?" he inquires while slamming the trunk of the Cutlass.

"I didn't know you were talking to me, being that I'm not a little girl."

I stop walking to engage him in conversation.

"Well, well, well. You finally figured it out, huh? Does your Grandmother know you're a grown ass woman now or am I the only one you trust with that information?" he quizzes me as he smiles while biting his bottom lip.

"I just want you to know." I declare, walking away again as he closely follows behind.

"Is that right, can I ask why?"

"Because I know you need me. Don't you need me, Brother Jenkings?" I ask while I turn to touch his hand.

"Oh wow, um, goddamn Sheela!" he stutters in response.

"Let me be your sex toy."

I wink at him before running towards the crowded lawn.

"Goddamn Sheela!" Brother Jenkings whispers loudly as he throws his hands on top of his head.

Chosen as my first gentleman, Brother Jenkings stands where I left him, considering the weight of his decision.

Hurrying to my grandmother, I quickly pass Sister Jenkings as she cackles with Sister Webb.

"Girl, look at him, he really needs to stop! You would think he's dying or something! It's just sex. Patience, brotha, patience."

Sister Jenkings continues to laugh with Sister Webb as they sit at their table staring in his direction.

Chapter 9

I consider the loss of my innocence watching the pretty little girls, once neatly groomed, roll in the grass of the empty lot. Brown and green impurities now stain their formerly pure white dresses as they play and fall, unbothered by the unavoidable slaps of discipline delivered by their mothers.

Brother Jenkings' eyes become distracted by my ass as I bend over to grab my grandmother's cooler. Commotion climbs from the group of men carrying tables inside the sanctuary as he nearly drops his end of the load.

I'm startled as a loud slapping noise followed by a stinging pain on my behind causes me to quickly stand and look for the source.

"You airhead! Why'd you ditch me this morning?" says Renada, in a demanding tone, still holding her hand in the air.

"I'm sorry, I slept in. Then I got caught in traffic on my way to buy a new outfit. Please let me make it up to you. I'll come get you tonight at 6:45."

Leaning in to give her a big hug and looking into her furious eyes, I knew she couldn't say no.

"Are you taking me to see *The Three Amigos* or something?"

"How'd you guess Renada?" I say, quickly claiming the idea. "But, there's one more surprise!"

"Is it a guy? You know I'm still trying to get over Brian."

Renada turns her lips into a frown as she looks at me with weepy eyes.

"Nope! Better. See you tonight."

I turn and grab the cooler.

"It's a date.", Renada responds before smiling and walking towards her car.

Hurrying to my grandmother's Cutlass, the sound of the gravel under my feet reminds me of my earlier conversation with Brother Jenkings. Opening the trunk, I cringe at the slightly opened clothing bags, still impressed by the shape of my body.

The erotic show I gave Brother Jenkings leaps to the front of my mind, and I shudder in embarrassment as I recall the scene.

"He probably thinks I'm crazy." I assume and I am disappointed.

Clenching my fist, I take a moment to drop my head and breathe deep, considering the humiliating possibilities I've created.

"Psst...I'm down."

I hear a deep voice whisper before smelling the scent of sweat and expensive cologne. I suppress my grin to Brother Jenkings as he slowly crosses behind me.

"Okay. Meet me at the 7:00 p.m. drive-in show tonight so we can talk." I command in a soft, almost breathless voice as he continues to walk away.

"I'll park next to the popcorn stand and flash my lights." he quietly responds, continuing to walk from my view.

My grandmother yearns for a shower and the comforts of her bed as I help her get into the car.

"I'm going to the 7:00 p.m. show with Renada so I'll be home late, okay Grandmother?" I say to her while buckling her seatbelt across her lap.

"Now that's good Sheela. Praise God for Renada. She is such a sweet girl. Okay, I'll see you later." she says, closing the door and placing keys into the ignition.

The engine on my grandmother's Cutlass growls as she accelerates from my view. I watch the shadows slowly consume the once bright blue sky, turning day into night. My body begins to feel anxious.

I can only think of Brother Jenkings' charming smile as I drive to my Aunt's house. I've never seen him outside of the sanctuary, but his enormous hands have always made me wonder what it would feel like to get him alone.

The street is dark as I pull in front of Aunt Khaki's house. The light from her television flashes through the front window, helping me to avoid the obstacles of overgrown grass and rocks along the narrow walk to her door.

"You really need to get a porch light and somebody to cut your grass.", I say, embracing her as I walk through the door.

The air in the house is hazy and dense with marijuana smoke. A cold spray of brown liquor hits my face as Uncle Ricky jumps from his seat and angrily yells at the television, tossing whiskey into the air.

"They should have flagged that play! These refs are sorrier than a mutha fucka. I swear before God if we lose this game I'm never watching Football again!", he shouts aggressively as he takes a seat in front of the television.

Using my arm to wipe the liquor from my face, I turn to

my Aunt for direction.

"Come on to my room, we don't need to be nowhere around Ricky right now."

Aunt Khaki pulls me through the hall into her room.

Falling onto the unfolded pile of laundry on her bed, I wait for her attention as she quickly finishes her duties.

Aunt Khaki opens the tightly sealed bag of Marijuana on her dresser and sniffs the inside.

Her wrist twists the buds through the teeth of the metal grinder before she sprinkles the grounded leaves into several white papers. Rolling and licking them closed one by one, she takes three joints from her room to Uncle Ricky.

The volume of the television roars through the cracked door as she quickly delivers his favors and gallops back to the bedroom. Taking a deep breath, Khaki selects a joint from the tray.

"What's up, Sheela? Momma getting on your nerves or something?"

She reclines against the dense pile of clothing before lighting the joint and passing it to me.

Recalling our last smoke session, I take a quick puff before passing it back.

"Well, Aunt Khaki, I need a favor. I wanted to know if you could give me a couple of joints to smoke with Renada. She's trying to get over her ex-boyfriend so I'm taking her to the drive-in tonight." I explain in my most innocent and desperate voice.

"Sure, tell her I said fuck that nigga." she advises as she rises from the bed to toss three joints into a small plastic sack.

"What time is the movie?"

She hands me the sack and looks at my bleach burned jeans.

"7:00 p.m., so I gotta run home and get ready."

I stand up and gesture towards the door.

"Just get ready here."

Khaki walks into her closet to return with a sleeveless yellow, polka dotted romper. It looks too small for either of us to fit, but I can tell it's meant to be that way.

"Oh my God!" I scream.

Escaping from my clothes and pulling the tiny romper over my thick legs and ass. The stretchy fabric snaps against my waist as I pull the top over my full breast.

Aunt Khaki pulls my fluffy curls into a high bun as I admire the adorable print of the fabric in the mirror, hardly able to contain my excitement.

"Okay girl! You look good. Don't let Momma get this one!" she states as she looks me up and down.

"I'll keep an outfit in my trunk." I respond, giving her a thumbs up, as she takes my hand to escort me to the front door.

The television volume rages and Uncle Ricky cheers as his team approaches victory. Aunt Khaki stops for a moment and admires me as we stand in the center of the room.

"Your Momma would have loved to see you, Sheela. You remind me so much of her. Sometimes it feels like I have my sister back again. Sometimes I wish it could've been me instead." she laments.

Uncle Ricky rudely interrupts and commands us to get out of his goddamn way. He's waving his hands and yelling that our asses are blocking the television.

Laughing to ourselves, we walk to the door to exchange a quick hug before I start towards the car.

"Have a good time!" yells Aunt Khaki from the porch, waving as I climb into my car.

I pause for a moment, watching the street light shine through my car window and move across my bare cleavage. Clinching the bag of joints and looking down at my sparsely covered body, I scream in excitement while enjoying the euphoric feeling of being half naked before driving to Renada's house.

Chapter 10

"You came. You're on time and your booty is out! What's the surprise?" Renada questions as she opens the car door, recoiling to look me up and down.

"Get in and close your eyes."

I smile as I remove one joint from the bag and place it in her hand. Feeling the strange weight, she slowly opens her eyes and gasps at the sight of the joint as I accelerate away from her house.

"We're about to smoke this before we go to the movies?" she asks, suppressing her nerves with a crooked smile.

"Yes, girl! It'll make the popcorn better." I say, parking in the driveway of the vacant house down the street.

I lift the joint to my lips and take the first pull, releasing the smoke into the confined space of my car. I take two more puffs before passing it to Renada. Her eyes are bucked in shock and her hand covers her mouth.

"Sheela! How many times have you done this?" she asks, impressed by the billowing clouds of smoke escaping from my lungs.

Through the haze of smoke, I watch Renada's hand move in slow motion to take the joint from my fingers. Putting the joint to her lips, she pulls the warm smoke into her lungs and coughs violently. Huffing large puffs of smoke from the air before struggling to roll down the window.

Clouds of marijuana smoke escape from the car as I laugh hysterically, rubbing Renada's back as she grips her throat and gasps for the clean fresh air through the window.

Sitting back into her seat and slowly cranking the window to a closed position, she burst into laughter.

"Oh my God, Sheela. Is this what they mean when they say stoned?"

Renada inquires through a wide grin; her eyes low and unsteady.

"I think so. We'll save the rest for the movie." I say backing out of the driveway onto the dark street.

My car seems to glide on the road and the mood is deep and meditative as we speak on the wonders of the world on our way to the theater.

"Park right there!" Renada yells, pointing to a space near the edge of the lot.

Gravel crunches under the tires as I park in the remote area. It's just beyond the view of the crowds, but close enough to see the movie screen.

Removing the small joint from the bag, I light the end, taking two puffs before passing it to Renada. The smoke in the air is illuminated by the small red light of the joint as she pulls the smoke into her lungs. She doesn't cough as she exhales a sparse cloud into the air and takes another puff.

"Oh, so you're a smoker now!" I say, laughing and clapping my hands in the air.

The quick flashing of headlights near the popcorn stand catches my eye and I feel weightless. Beads of sweat quickly stack against my brow as I anticipate the moment I reach Brother Jenkings car. I feel rude for making him wait as he flashes his lights again and slightly rolls down the window, exposing only the tip of his cigarette.

"Do you want some popcorn?" I ask Renada as she stares into space, unconsciously finishing the joint.

"That sounds so good right now. And get a drink too. I'm super thirsty.", she responds before returning to her reclined position. The car door slams behind me as I begin the walk towards Brother Jenkings' Cadillac DeVille. The yellow lights from the popcorn stand reflect from the burgundy paint, and I'm beginning to see his silhouette through the windshield. He cracks his door to extinguish his cigarette before closing it again.

I quickly approach the passenger door and slide into the seat. Smiling towards him as he stares in my direction.

The air in the sedan is cold, and the leather seats are chilled. Goosebumps rise across my exposed skin as it touches the cool surface. I rub my hands across my legs and ask him to make it warmer as I try to get comfortable.

"Goddamn Sheela! You look good as a mutha fucka." Brother Jenkings says to me before reaching towards the knobs on the dashboard.

"I've never heard you speak like that before." I say, giggling and still rubbing the chill from my legs.

"Well, I've never really seen you before, have I?" he questions me, fixing his eyes on my smooth skin and the generous curves accentuated by my romper.

Except for the faint sound of a love song, there's a moment of silence in the car. It would be awkward if it weren't for the sexual tension between us. The scent of his cologne mixed with the sweet smell of Cadillac leather is intoxicating, and I'm turned on by the way he handles his cigarettes. Tapping the end before lighting it, gently holding it between his fingers, placing it softly between his lips and sucking, then blowing.

He closes the small gap in the window and relaxes into the comfortable seat before turning his head towards me.

"Give me your hand, Sheela." Brother Jenkings says, gently laying his hand on the seat beside me.

"Do you know what we're doing?" he questions as he softly clinches his large hand around mine.

His inquiry is briefly lost in my mind as the marijuana takes my head higher. Unconscious of the time I'm taking to respond, I stare at him, my heart rate increasing.

Raindrops, slowly then quickly, fall onto the roof of the car, joining to form thick sheets of water that blanket the windows.

"What do you want this to be?" I eventually respond, causing Brother Jenkings to lift from his slouched position.

I can hear the sadness in his voice as he tries several times to make sense of his decision.

"Two years is a long time for a man Sheela. My wife is beautiful, but she won't let me see her. She definitely doesn't think I'm attractive or how else could she go through life not fucking me. I just need to feel like a man. Like I felt before."

Brother Jenkings stops for a moment, looking down at my thighs, hypnotized by the moving shadows the rain creates across my lap.

"I'm so frustrated, Sheela and you're so fine. And, your skin is so soft. I need you, but are we ready for this?"

Brother Jenkings nervously pulls his lips into his mouth before rubbing his hands over his head and reclining back into the seat.

The sound of the rain continues to lull us into thought as we contemplate our next move. My imagination takes me to wild places and my legs fold onto the seat to crawl towards Brother Jenkings lap.

"Are you a virgin, Sheela?", Brother Jenkings asks as I

straddle his waist and look into his eyes.

"Yes. You'll be my first, but don't worry, I've been planning for you." I say, placing his smooth face between my breast and softly kissing the top of his bald head.

"How've you been planning for me, Sheela?"

He talks as I continue to kiss him gently across his neck.

Brother Jenkings body grows hot and I feel tension in the crotch of his pants. Slowly moving my hand down his torso, I grip the source and it gets harder.

Our eyes meet and his tongue enters my mouth, gently caressing the inside as he positions my back against the steering wheel. Softly kissing down my chest.

My romper slips, exposing my breast through the top. Brother Jenkings sucks on my nipples and the Cadillac rocks as I continue to grip and grind against the firm knot between his legs. Panting together, we fog the windows, moaning and touching each other.

"I'm about to nut, Sheela", says Brother Jenkings, gripping my waist and firmly grinding my body against his swollen crotch.

After several strokes, he moans loudly in pleasure and ejaculates semen into his pants.

We sit in silence as the raindrops slow to a drizzle and the blanket of water that once hid our passion breaks.

Slowly climbing from his lap, I fix my romper and use the mirror to check my face before turning to look at him. The way his hand grips the firm mound inside his pants makes me want to finish, but I can see my car from here.

"I have to head out now, but come see me tomorrow night. Just knock three times on my window and I'll be ready."

I instruct him before opening the door and stepping from

the car, still tingling all over from our session.

"I can dig it." he says, tilting his head upward and licking his lips in my direction.

Brother Jenkings flashes his lights to let me know he's watching as I purchase refreshments and walk back to my car.

Renada snores loudly in the passenger seat as I light the small joint she saved in the tray. A smoky haze fills the car, and she coughs, waking from her slumber. Reaching through the cloud of smoke, I pass her the joint and she accepts it from my fingertips. She takes a puff before reaching her hand in the bucket of popcorn and staring through the haze at the movie screen.

"Did you get wet?" she asks, shoving a handful of kernels into her mouth.

"Yes, very." I say, laughing to myself.

Chapter 11

My room is dimly lit as I lick my finger and quickly flip through the pages of my momma's book. After only a moment of study, I use a blade to slice a marijuana joint down the side. Dumping the innards into a small mason jar, I carefully pour hot butter over the crushed leaves and strike a match to light a large vanilla scented candle near my window seal.

Herbs steep in butter swish in a circular motion as I hover the mason jar over the flame. I inhale deeply as a familiar aroma wafts through the air. My stocking strains bits of herbs from the butter and my fingers burn as it drips into a second jar filled with chocolate chips. I stir the sweet concoction with a wooden spoon before referring to the book, reading it for instruction.

> *Speak this prayer into the jar before cooling the chocolate.*
> *Daughter of the River. Goddess of Love. Golden one whose taste is honey and whose touch is the flow of water. Bless us with your ability to Love. Ase.*

Turning from the book, I grab the jar and whisper the prayer before drizzling the melted chocolate onto a tray lined with wax paper. I fold the cooled sheet of chocolate into an envelope, breaking it into pieces, before placing it next to a jar of honey sitting by my mirror.

I arrange a yellow candle on my dresser and lay a white silk gown on my reading chair. A cassette tape labeled *Love Songs* sits in the player next to my cinnamon incense.

AMIYA CLEVELAND

Erotic sensations swallow my body as I fantasize about my upcoming session with Brother Jenkings. I can hardly wait to hear those three knocks.

Walking from my room and closing the door, I twirl into the kitchen to greet Grandmother eating breakfast.

"Good Morning, Grandmother. Wish me luck on my final exams today. Nurse Mitchell has been really hard on us lately.", I explain as I kiss her cheek before turning to walk towards the front door.

"I'm sure she'll get you all out of there early. We're riding to a funeral in Waco this evening, and we'll be out there until tomorrow."

Grandmother continues to eat her breakfast after delivering this news.

"Ah, man! How come you didn't tell me, Grandmother? I would have been so worried about you." I say in a disappointed tone.

"Ain't nobody thinking about you, Sheela. I'll call you when I get settled."

Grandmother laughs to herself as I walk out the door.

The only sound comes from Nurse Mitchells' pen scratching against the paper as the class sits at attention in the simulation room.

Pulling on a gray wig, Renada lies on the hospital bed, pretending to be a patient, telling me a scripted story as I take her vital signs.

"I can't stop throwing up, I think the medicine the other nurse gave me is helping a bit, but I still feel fatigue." Renada acts in a weak voice and struggles to keep her eyes open.

I comfort her before tightening the cuff around her arm and releasing the air. Stopping to make notes before inserting a thermometer into her mouth and watching the mercury rise.

A few moments pass and my heart pounds as I hear the scratch of Nurse Mitchell's pen against the paper.

"98.2, normal."

I reach for my stethoscope before wiping the sweat from my brow.

"You're doing great." compliments Renada, looking at me from the corner of her eyes.

Releasing a deep breath, I thank her silently before continuing.

"Let me take a quick listen to your belly. Are you having bowel movements?"

I lift Renada's gown and place the stethoscope on her abdomen as I continue the examination.

"Yes, Nurse, I pooped earlier."

"Ok, good, but I hear a lot of gurgling. Is there any pain when I press down?" I ask, firmly pressing my fingers into her side.

"Ouch, yes!", she yells, rolling over in the bed.

"Hold still. I'm almost done.", I say in a calm, professional voice while pulling her back onto the pillow.

"Let's check your hydration."

I grab a small section of Renada's skin from her upper arm and pinch.

"I noticed it took some time for your skin to bounce back to normal. You're definitely dehydrated. I'll order an IV." I say, making a note on my clipboard before looking back at my patient.

"Do you smoke?" I question, suppressing a grin as I stare

into her eyes.

"No." Renada answers, choking back her laugh.

"Perfect." I say, winking my eye and continuing to make notes.

Nurse Mitchell instructs us to return to our seats as she writes in her book. Our heels click towards the back of the class and we stand to watch the next pair take their turn.

One at a time, pairs of students approach the simulation area to perform their mock exams and be graded by Nurse Mitchell.

She strikes several red marks across the grade sheets of one girl who forgot her stethoscope and two others who simply froze, unable to perform under pressure. Renada and I gasp from the back of the class as they're unemotionally dismissed as failures.

"Alright. To those of you who made it, I'd like to say congratulations. The graduation ceremony will be in two weeks. Please drop all keys and medical gear in the designated bins as you walk through the door." Nurse Mitchell says, suppressing heartfelt emotion under her stern demeanor.

Hugs are exchanged by the class as we quickly sort our belongings and prepare to leave. My key to the simulation room stares at me from the bottom of my backpack, and I can't bring myself to give it back. This room is soon to be vacant and I may need it, at least for a while.

The students drop medical gear and keys into designated buckets as we all gently hug Nurse Mitchell and walk through the door. My key softly scratches against the bottom of my backpack as I quickly hug and hurry past her, hoping she won't stop to remind me of my neglect.

A heavy anxiousness hangs over my body as I pull away

from the school. The weight of my sin is heavy on my heart, but still too sweet to give up.

I arrive home and trudge up the steep drive. There's a note taped to the front door and my mind clears as I unfold the paper, looking to understand the words.

I came by again. Hopefully, God will put it on your heart to allow me to see her. I'm sorry and I need Sheela to forgive me. Signed, Marvin.

I read from the note before pushing through the door.

Squinting my eyes in confusion, I place the letter on the kitchen table to wait for Grandmother. I wonder why I need to forgive him. I've never heard of anyone named Marvin.

Entering my room and removing my clothes, I fall between the comfortable mounds of pillows on the bed. My momma's book joins me under the covers.

Running my finger along the pages, I read an underlined passage,

> *Daughter of Sweet Water, giver of love. Be careful not to allow emotional binding with your gentleman. He must focus on his wife during the healing session.*

I stop for a moment, concerned and noticing the dimness of the sunlight. I question myself why I haven't heard from my grandmother as I run into the kitchen, grabbing the phone just as it rings. I'm relieved as my grandmother's voice speaks immediately from the other line.

"Hey Sheela, I'm already in Waco. I met Nurse Mitchell at the school and we left from there. I'll see you tomorrow afternoon, okay?"

She appears to be in a good mood and I can hear her laughing in casual conversation with someone in the background.

"It's so good to hear from you. Thanks for letting me know Grandmother. By the way, who's Marvin? I ask, smiling into the phone.

"Alright baby, see you later."

Grandmother clears her throat and quickly releases the line.

Chapter 12

It's 1:00 a.m. and the house is completely silent. I wait anxiously as every car that passes sounds as if it should be followed by three knocks.

My skin reflects the light of scented candles as I relax on the floor, comforted by several white blankets. I stare at the yellow candle on my dresser and imagine how I will use it soon.

Time passes and I almost nod off as headlights flash across my room, my heart races and I climb from the ground, quickly pressing play on my cassette player and fixing my hair. The soft sound of crunching grass precedes three knocks on my window. I nervously open it to see Brother Jenkings standing in wait.

"So, are you going to let me in or what?"

Brother Jenkings smiles as I release the small fire escape ladder.

His familiar scent fills my room as he explores, admiring the comfortable surroundings, gripping my pillows and running his fingers firmly across the tender cotton sheets on my bed. He turns his eyes towards the layered blankets and tray of confections in front of my mirror.

"Is that for me?" he asks, smiling and removing his shirt as he walks in my direction.

"Yes, it is. Get comfortable. But before we start, there's only one rule for you." I explain as he embraces my waist and kisses my neck.

"You have to remember we are here to strengthen your marriage."

"I can dig it, Sheela." he confirms as he rubs his hands across my ass before lifting and carrying me to the blankets.

Caressing my body through my gown, he spreads my legs. Dipping his head to move my panties to the side and lick his tongue in between.

"You taste good." says Brother Jenkings, lifting to look at the expression of ecstasy on my face.

I'm reminded that this is a healing session as the corners of my Momma's book slightly peek from beneath the mattress. I move my body away from his lips and stand on the blankets as he kneels in front of me.

"Let's slow down."

I slowly remove my gown before allowing him to make the next move.

He smiles at me while slowly removing the clothes from his fit body.

"Is that slow enough?" he asks, placing his hands around my face and kissing my mouth.

"Let's sit on the ground."

Brother Jenkings looks at me questionably as I guide him downward. Folding my legs against the blanket, we sit across from one another.

"Tell me how you need to feel."

I say, staring directly into his eyes.

"I need to feel like a man." he says as I slowly crawl over and place my hands against his inner thighs.

Kissing him across his chest, I speak over him that he is a man while gripping his manhood. I move to sit on his lap, straddling his waist and gripping it with folded legs. Hugging him tightly as his hands rub softly across my back, our genitals press firmly together.

"Do you like chocolate?" I probe, leaning to look at him.

"Yes."

Gripping my waist, Brother Jenkings lowers me onto the floor.

I grab a piece of chocolate from the envelope and put it between my lips while climbing to my knees. I hold my hands behind my back and silently invite him to take the chocolate from my mouth.

He joins me, putting his lips over mine and sucking the chocolate into his mouth.

"What's that peppery flavor?" he asks, licking his lips.

"Herbed oil." I explain before placing my fingers into the jar of honey.

Sticky sweetness drips onto the blankets as I gently massage honey onto my private parts. Brother Jenkings licks his lips and reclines against his elbow, watching me while stroking himself.

"Come taste." I say, removing my fingers and placing my hands behind my back. Without delay, he rises, grabbing my thighs and placing his head between them.

His lips touch my body, and his tongue extends, flicking and sucking my clit softly until all the honey is gone.

Euphoric tingles cover me as his tongue induces a wave of ecstasy up my spine. My encounter with Brother Jenkings is forever cemented in my memory as I yell out to God in pleasure. My body goes limp, and he catches me, gently laying me onto the ground.

I allow him to spread my legs and he positions himself between them. I recoil slightly as he gently presses his phallus against my wet vagina, finding the entry to my womb and threatening to slip inside.

"Are you ready, Sheela?" he cautiously asks.

"Yes." I whisper as he presses the tip of his manhood against me.

I relax my body as it opens, stretching tightly around Brother Jenkings firm penis. Inch by inch, he slips inside until I'm filled completely.

I feel the painful pinch of lost innocence as he exclaims in pleasure. The sound of my wetness smacks and his penis grows harder as he continues to grind against me. Sweat rolls down his body and his mouth hangs open as my vagina squeezes him tightly.

"You feel so good.", he exclaims, looking down before closing his eyes and tilting his head back.

Grabbing my ass, he slightly lifts me from the ground and thrusts faster. The pleasurable feeling of his penis softens the stinging pain and I allow him to take control. The rhythm of his stroke changes and he trembles.

"Sheela, I'm about to cum." Brother Jenkings says passionately, looking between my thighs as he continues to push himself in and out.

"Put it on my stomach." I request, afraid to allow it into my yoni as instructed in the recipe, as he pulls back to remove his penis and quickly stroke the shaft until thick white streams shoot from the tip.

"Fuck!" he yells as the white river pools on top of me.

In shock, I'm frozen on the blanket, staring at the snot like substance that is quickly cooling on my belly.

"Where are the towels?" asks Brother Jenkings, still holding his pulsing manhood.

"They're in the hall by the bathroom. Don't worry. No one is here." I tell him as he opens my bedroom door, peeking his head out before walking naked down the hall.

I jump from the blanket, quickly tipping towards the yellow candle on the dresser to scrape the ejaculate from my belly onto the wax. Lighting it, I take a deep breath, trying to remember the spell, before whispering over the flame.

"Our bond is...uh fuck...open? Tonight was very nice. Now return this love to your wife?" I say, panicked, and only once as I question my accuracy.

Placing the candle back on the dresser, I scramble back to my position with only a few seconds to spare as Brother Jenkings returns with two wet towels. Taking one from his hand, we look at each other, mentally reviewing our act as we wipe the sex and honey from our bodies.

"Do you feel like a man?" I ask, looking at him while rubbing the towel between my legs.

"Baby, you can call me Mr. Tee." he says playfully, noticing the soft flickering light of the yellow candle.

"You must be ready for round two." Brother Jenkings comments as he licks his lips in my direction.

"Round two is for your wife. I'll see you in 28 days"

I giggle as I return the gown to my body.

"Yeah, right. I'll see you in 28 days." he announces, looking at the clock as he quickly puts on his shoes.

Brother Jenkings and I exchange a brief kiss as he backs down my fire escape. I enjoy the sound of the crunching grass as he walks from my view. His headlights flash through my window, highlighting my skin as I sit, satisfied and smiling to myself on the stained white blankets.

Chapter 13

Sunday service is a little different now. I can see Brother Jenkings watching me and he looks bothered when I speak to other men in the congregation.

I've just finished thanking Pastor Webb for his inspiring message as Brother Jenkings hurries past me whispering,

"When's the next time?" looking back for an answer before taking a seat next to his wife.

It's been three weeks since our first session and we've been together once since then, but I can still feel his body calling me.

Sister Jenkings doesn't notice. She smiles in contentment as he sits close and holds her hand. Sliding his arm around her shoulder, he listens attentively to something she wants to share as they exchange giggles. I'm happy knowing I've helped their marriage, but I can't help but notice the way he keeps looking for me.

We shouldn't do it again, at least until the 28 days are up.

The sound of Brother Marcus' baritone voice gets my attention and makes me wonder if his dark, smooth skin continues from his face to the rest of his body. Slowly moving towards a clamoring crowd in the center of the sanctuary, I admire his groomed beard and clean haircut. Maybe I'll get close enough to smell his soft, yet masculine perfume.

"Us, next!" says Sister Marcus while gripping Brother Marcus around the waist and positioning him in front of the camera.

"Such a handsome couple." the photographer notices before taking their photograph.

Releasing her pose, Sister Marcus shimmies back into the crowd, joining a group of Sisters who are laughing and gossiping at the rear. Brother Marcus pleads with her for brevity as she settles in with her companions. Taking a seat on an empty pew and flipping through his Bible, he patiently waits for his wife.

His ankle crosses his knee and my eyes fix on the bulge between his legs as I walk toward him.

"Thanks for coming to my graduation!" I acknowledge as Brother Marcus shifts his position to face me.

"My pleasure, Sheela. Nursing fits you very well, and so does the uniform." he comments, shaking his head as his eyes admire my body.

"Well, I can be your nurse. Just let me know when you want to play." I whisper.

Startled, Brother Marcus stands from his seat and looks around for his wife.

"Whoa! I was just being flirtatious, but I'll have to get back to you on that."

Brother Marcus laughs nervously as he stares at me with a mischievous smile.

"No rush." I confirm, returning the grin.

As I walk towards the exit doors, I quicken my pace. I can feel eyes watching from the dark corner by the men's room. My hand briefly touches the latch on the exit door before I hear Christian's voice.

"So, what was that about Sheela? You're just passing it out now."

Christian leaps from the shadows and joins me on my

walk. Looking at him only to roll my eyes, we push through the door as I keep my stride to the parking lot.

"You know, it could be dangerous, talking to those married men the way you do. What if someone was to hear you other than me?" he states, grabbing my arm to slow me down.

"Seriously? Christian, you are such a hypocrite. My ears are constantly burning with stories about you. I can't believe you would try to lecture me." I say as I snatch my arm before stopping to look at him.

"Look, Sheela, I'm sorry. I wish that I would have waited for you. But I just want you to know you're worth more than this."

Christian stares sincerely into my eyes and I grow angry, remembering for a moment how it felt when he broke my heart.

"Worth more than what? What am I doing? Just quit spying on me, Christian." I say, walking away.

"I wasn't spying on you. I just want to be here for you."

Christian walks swiftly to join me.

"Whatever. Listening to my private conversations then judging me is not cool." I yell as I enter my car and lock the door.

The passenger door flies open and Christian jumps inside, slamming the door and glaring at me. After a moment, he touches my hand softly and the mood calms. Our fingers wrap around each other, making a fist as he pulls me closer, holding me tight in his arms. He's warm and his heart is pounding. I lift my head and our lips meet. We share a simple kiss before I push away, sliding back into my seat.

"Please, Sheela. Let's give it a shot.", he says looking longingly at me. His lips still wet from our kiss.

"I can't. My mind is focused on other things right now."
I explain while turning to look at him.

"The things you're focused on will probably get you pregnant." Christian declares under his breath, snatching his hand from the seat while making a fist.

"What about your other girls? I know at least one of them has to be pregnant by now." I say, rolling my eyes as I fasten my seat belt.

"That's some bullshit. I'm outta here." Christian says, reaching for the door handle before turning to look at me.

Correcting my posture, I turn the key in the ignition and look forward as though I am ready to leave.

"Alright, go be a whore then!" he yells before jumping out of the car and slamming the door.

"Takes one to know one!" I yell back through the glass before speeding from the lot.

It's strange that my grandmother beat me home today, but even more strange to see Sister Webb sitting at the kitchen table. I overhear my Grandmother say, "That bastard doesn't deserve to have a daughter." before quickly hiding a piece of paper behind her back.

Slowly walking into the kitchen to join them, I ask, "What's going on, did something happen?"

My eyes race quickly back at fourth between them.

"It's nothing Sheela, just God's business. Sister Webb is here to help me figure it out. Gone back yonder until we're through." Grandmother commands gesturing towards the back of the house.

"Yes, Grandmother." I say, turning to walk towards my

room.

"Have you been enjoying the women's meetings, Sheela?" asks Sister Webb.

"Yes ma'am." I state, briefly stopping to look in her direction.

"Well, I look forward to seeing you tomorrow."

I can tell she's watching me walk away. Her eyes were full of pity and I know she's hiding something that's mine.

I can't get to my room fast enough as they wait for the door to slam behind me.

Pacing angrily, warm tears fall into my mouth as I cry in frustration. Dense pillows fly from my bed as I hurl them into empty corners. The thought of Sister Webb and my grand-mother speaking about me in secret causes rage to build inside of me. They don't have the right to judge me or keep secrets. Who I am and what I need to know is my business, not my grandmother's.

I can hear muffled laughs from the kitchen as I burst through my bedroom door.

"I'm sick of this! Who's father is he? Mine, yours, my Momma's. It's so many missing daddies in this family I can barely keep up!"

I yell as I march into the kitchen, demanding answers from Grandmother and Sister Webb.

"Now you hold on one goddamn minute, Sheela Diggs. You demand nothing from me in my house." my grandmother responds angrily, standing to meet me.

"I'm tired of the secrets! You're constantly talking about how promiscuous my Momma was and telling me I don't have a father, but if Marvin is my daddy or grandfather, I need to know and I want to know right now."

Full of rage, I only pause for a moment before Sister Webb stands to softly grab my shoulders.

"Oh, so you done got a whiff of your own piss huh, Sheela? How are you gonna make me tell you who Marvin is?" my grandmother asks in a threatening tone.

"This is ridiculous! I shouldn't have to make you tell me Grandmother; you're a Christian."

Staring squarely into her eyes, she delivers a firm back-hand slap across my cheek. Blood leaks from my lip as I grab my face.

Sister Webb reacts in shock, gasping loudly before moving in between us, blocking additional blows from hitting me.

"It's none of your goddamn business, Sheela. But I'll tell you right now, if you say one more word, you'll leave my house and never look back."

My grandmother insists, pointing her finger at me over Sister Webb's shoulder.

"You're such a hypocrite, Grandmother! Hitting me and holding secrets like this. Would it hurt to let me know where I come from?" I cry into Sister Webb's back, staining her dress with blood.

"You're just like your Momma. As stupid as they come. Get your ass out of my house!" Grandmother yells, pushing around Sister Webb as she walks toward my room.

"Don't worry about it. I'll help her." Sister Webb states as she grabs my grandmother's arm, pulling her back into the kitchen.

"Fine. As long as it's done in a hurry. I've been sick of this girl since her Momma put her on me."

My grandmother snatches her arm from Sister Webb before walking into her room and slamming the door.

"Who is Marvin?" I scream through my grandmother's door before looking to Sister Webb for answers.

"I'll tell you everything I know. Just come stay with me for a while." she whispers, using a napkin to dab the blood from my face while escorting me to my room.

Chapter 14

The car ride feels long and the only sound is from my bags sliding across the tiny backseat of Sister Webb's coupe as we cross several roads and bridges.

"Are you okay?" asks Sister Webb.

I quietly nod my head in her direction before turning to look out the window at the winding roads.

I choose not to speak. There's a large knot in my throat and every time I open my mouth, it threatens to cause a flood of tears.

The smile of a tall security guard, dressed in all black greets us before he opens the mechanical gate surrounding Sister Webb's gated neighborhood. Each home is a paradise-themed mansion featuring floor to ceiling windows and several green acres of land. The shrubs are perfectly manicured by a gardener who waves as we pass. Every driveway has at least two luxury cars.

"Almost there." Sister Webb assures me as we turn a sharp corner.

Soon we approach a white stone mansion with a fountain and small garden in the middle of the drive.

These homes... I think to myself as I'm hypnotized by my luxurious surroundings.

Smiling in my direction, she pulls through her covered driveway and parks her car between a black Mercedes and a blue Cadillac.

"Be careful not to hit Pastor Webb's toys with the car

door." she warns, laughing for a moment before unlocking the door.

I grab my bags from the seat and quickly follow her up the stone walk to the breezeway. Leaning on the heavy, unlocked door and pushing it open, we step through the foyer onto cream marble floors.

The air smells like hardwood, new carpet, and chlorine. A spiral staircase leads to a bridge between the east and west wings of the house. I can hear the steady trickling of a waterfall running into her tropical pool. There's a small guest house tucked neatly at the rear of the island escape.

"This is a really beautiful home." I comment.

"It's no big deal." She says, shrugging her shoulders as she grabs my bags.

"You'll be staying in the guest house, but I want you in the main house with us as much as possible. Your grandmother needs a break, and we can help you heal."

Sister Webb walks lightly over the classic marble floors through the sliding glass doors.

The birds are singing, and the sun reflects off the pool. I stop for a second to dip my fingers into the cool water as Sister Webb opens the door to a perfectly decorated apartment. It smells of white cotton with designs decorated in pink and gray. Sun shines through the windows, scattering reflective sparkles across the plush furniture, allowing me to admire the beautiful arrangement.

"Did you do this yourself?" I say as Sister Webb takes blankets and pillows from a hall closet and places them on the bed.

"Yes ma'am. I'll give you a moment to get settled and we'll talk after dinner."

Looking concerned, Sister Webb prepares to leave the guest house.

"Thank you for having me. Please let me know if there is anything I can do for you or Pastor while I'm here."

I place my bags on the couch and prepare to unpack.

"Bless your heart. I'll definitely let you know." she says, smiling and closing the door, leaving me in a brief silence.

A loud ring startles me. I look up to see Sister Webb holding a phone and waving her hand at me through the windows of the main house.

Running to find the phone, I quickly answer to hear her chipper voice on the other end.

"If we need anything, we can just call you from the main house. I just wanted to tell you that dinner will be ready at 7:30pm.,"

"Got it. See you then."

I return her smiley disposition as I disconnect the line.

The shower fogs the bathroom mirror as I stare at the split in my swollen lip. My mind wonders how my grandmother could be so cruel to someone who has never caused her any pain. Desperate, I try to reason with myself and imagine forgiving her, but my heart turns cold at the thought.

My body enters the tub as warm water gently pours from the shower head. I rub soap into a loofah before slowly massaging it across my skin. The rich soap covers me in a sugar scent as thick lather falls in satisfying sheets into the tub.

There's a small window letting in just enough sun as I

bathe myself in the comfortable dim light and dance to sweet music on the radio.

Taking my time, I lather and rinse well before leaving the shower.

A fresh cotton robe hangs on a hook behind the bathroom door. Sliding it on, I enjoy the luxurious feel before walking into the kitchen for a glass of water. Startled by a shadowy figure, I jump, spilling water all over myself.

"You've already settled in, I see." says Pastor Webb, adjusting the cuffs of his blue velvet jacket while staring at me.

"Pastor Webb, I'm sorry, I didn't hear you knock." I announce apologetically brushing water from my robe.

"I didn't. I don't knock on doors in my house Sheela." he arrogantly smiles in my direction.

"Oh, I see."

I laugh to myself thinking of his smart ass response.

"So, how long do you plan on staying?"

The heels of his alligator shoes click against the wooden floor as he takes a few steps in my direction.

"Not for long. I'll interview at a few hospitals and hopefully have a job in a couple of weeks. I should be able to afford something on Berri Street with my first month's pay."

"Berri Street? Aim higher, baby. Take your time. Just help Sister Webb with her responsibilities. As long as you can keep her happy, you can stay."

He winks before turning to walk to the door.

"Thanks, Pastor Webb. I'm here if you need me."

He turns to look at me, giving me an eye I'm beginning to recognize.

"Just focus on Sister Webb. Don't forget, dinner's at 7:30 p.m." he says, closing the door behind himself.

Chapter 15

Sister Webb admires my promptness as I approach the dinner table. Sliding into my seat, I compliment the neatness of the table she's set with fine china and crystal.

"Would you like red or white?" she asks, standing over me, holding a wine bottle in each hand.

"I've never had either." I respond while shrugging my shoulders.

"Well, we're having a casserole tonight, so let's go with the red wine."

She pours generously into my glass.

Pastor Webb sits in the seat across from me, reading a Christian newspaper.

"Would you like some wine, Honey?" she asks.

Not waiting for a response, she pours red wine into his glass and quickly disappears back into the kitchen.

My stomach growls as I try to distract myself by admiring the beautiful centerpiece. Tall white flowers at the end of bright green stalks sit perfectly between several springs of baby's breath. The linens are professionally cleaned and pressed, and the silver is polished immaculately.

Sister Webb emerges from the kitchen with a rolling tray and neatly sets our dinner plates, pre-served with an ample portion of casserole, along with a basket of yeast rolls on the table.

"Happy eating." Sister Webb cheerfully announces as she takes her seat while neatly placing a napkin across her lap.

"Pastor, please bless the food?" she requests, outstretching her hand and lowering her head.

Folding his newspaper, he looks up at both of us and after a few awkward moments, asks us to bow our heads. I can't help but to peek at them, noticing the lack of excitement as he delivers the blessing over the food. I begin to feel anxious at the thought of eating something unsavory and reacting in disgust. I need to keep Sister Webb happy, and I don't want to offend her in her home.

"Amen" we all say in unison as we place our forks into the mound of casserole before us.

"I hope you enjoy it, Sheela. It's my mother's recipe."

Sister Webb takes a spoonful of the dish, blowing on it slightly to cool before placing it in her mouth. Shivering and wincing as she swallows.

Pastor Webb takes a moment, staring down into the food before him, as he takes a deep breath and scoops a bite into his mouth. Swallowing it whole without chewing and chasing it with several gulps of water.

Curious, I take a small portion of the casserole onto my fork. The sharp twinge of an over-salted base and a strange bitterness triggers my gag reflex. The pasta has melted into the separated watery cream and the bite of raw chopped onions contrast the chalky overcooked chicken. Every layer is spoiled, nothing close to edible.

Grabbing a roll from the basket, I bite down and it knocks against my teeth, releasing a dry powder into my throat. Coughing, I grab my glass of wine. Turning it up and drinking until I rinse all of the flavor from my mouth. Out of breath, I place the empty glass on the table and notice Sister Webb staring at me.

"Is everything okay, Sheela?" she asks while taking another small bite of the casserole.

"Oh, I'm alright. I think I'm just a little upset about everything that happened today. I had a fight with Christian and of course you already know about my grandmother." I acknowledge, pretending to be sad and placing my fork on the table.

"Oh yes, I definitely understand. Do you want to talk about your fight with Christian? You know that's my little buddy." Sister Webb questions as if she is looking for some pleasant dinner conversation.

Pastor Webb shakes his head, looking disgusted as he wipes his lips and places a napkin across his mound of uneaten casserole. His eyes turn interestingly in my direction, encouraging me to speak.

I can't possibly share the truth about my argument with Christian. Telling them I'm pissed because he caught me making perverted suggestions to Brother Marcus would cause too much disapproval.

"Well, Christian and I have been best friends or play cousins our entire lives. He's still really important to me, but we seem to think in two different directions. It gets weird sometimes and we don't have enough time for each other."

I take a sip of water, choking down this not so truthful revelation.

"Are you and Christian dating?" Pastor Webb asks, tilting down his glasses and giving me a very nosy expression.

"No, never. I don't want to ruin what we have."

"I understand, dear." says Sister Webb, taking another bite from her plate.

"Well, is there anyone that you are interested in? Will there be any young man or young woman visiting us while you're here?", she questions, winking her eye at me.

Brother Jenking's face runs through my mind.

"Nope. I'll just be helping you and searching for an apartment while I'm here. Hopefully, it won't take me too long."

I continue to fill my belly with another sip of water.

"Well, I'll definitely appreciate the help. Do you do any cooking?" Sister Webb asks.

"Yes!" I exclaim, jumping from my seat. "I can do all the cooking if you like." I offer, watching them smile as if I have answered a prayer.

We all laugh and openly discuss how bad the casserole is as Sister Webb pours more wine into our glasses.

"If you guys are hungry, I could whip up something right now."

I look back-and-forth between them as they happily accept my offer and I hurry into the kitchen.

The pantry and the refrigerator are sparse. Only a few pieces of chicken and an uncovered bit of bread dough sit on the counter. Three yams lay near a cutting board, and I find a jar of honey sitting on the window ledge near a box of tea.

I generously season the chicken and dredge it in white flour before frying to a golden brown. Steam and sweet aromas escape a small pot of diced yams I've topped with sugar and cinnamon. I bake the bits of dough into fluffy rolls and slather butter across each piece before adding them alongside the plated chicken and yams. Warm honey drips from the jar as I drizzle it over each plate and happily present to the Webb's.

The click of forks against the plate is the only sound as they consume everything in silence.

Finally full and satisfied, they open their eyes towards me and express gratitude for providing such a wonderful dinner.

"Oh no, I couldn't." I declare to Sister Webb as she tries to pour another glass of wine for me.

"Just relax. You can sleep in tomorrow."

She laughs as she sips from her glass.

She and Pastor Webb laugh as they retell stories about their younger years, reminiscing about the '60s and how they had been just like me. Their dramatic hand gestures turn to fuzzy blobs of light as my vision blurs. My speech slurs as I push from the table, asking to be excused.

"Are you all right, Sheela?" asks Sister Webb.

"Yes, but I think the red wine is getting to me."

I'm dizzy and holding onto the table, trying not to fall.

"Oh dear, I'm sorry! Let me help you."

Sister Webb gets up from her seat.

"I'll be right back, honey." she tells Pastor Webb as she escorts me to the guest house.

I fall onto the bed and feel a dense blanket placed on top of me. Sister Webb moves my hair from my face before saying good night. My eyes slightly open and I see her watching over me as I drift into a deep slumber.

Chapter 16

The loud ringing of the phone jolts me from my sleep. The pressure in my head is increased by the glare of the sunlight. I cover my head with the blanket as the phone continues to ring.

"All right! All right!" I say, jumping from the bed and grabbing the phone.

"This is Sheela, how can I help you?"

My voice is dry and scratchy as I wait to hear a response from the caller.

"Sheela! Oh my God! I can't believe that you live with Sister Webb now!"

Renada screams into the phone while laughing hysterically on the other end of the line.

"Your grandmother told my grandmother you went crazy and walked out of the house." she says, quieting her laugh to wait for a response.

"Did she tell her she slapped me in front of Sister Webb?" I ask, furiously twisting the phone cord in my hand.

"Girl! No!" Renada says in shock.

"Well, she did. Got blood on Sister Webb's dress and everything, just because I wanted to know who some guy named Marvin is. On the bright side, it's really nice at Pastor Webb's house. I have my own apartment and they let me cook. I finally had a glass of wine and we had a great dinner conversation. They're more open than you would think! Maybe they can help me be a better person."

Renada listens intently on the other end.

"Marvin? That name sounds familiar, but maybe I'm thinking about Marvin Gaye. Well, I love you and I only want the best for you, even if that means not living down the street from each other anymore."

Renada's voice cracks with emotion.

"I love you too, Renada. Thanks for checking on me."

I send Renada a kiss through the phone.

A clicking sound followed by silence echoes from the other end of the line.

"Renada, are you still there?" I ask, listening for her voice.

"Yeah, I'm still here. What was that?"

"I'm not sure. I'll call you back a little later."

I look from my window into the main house as I disconnect the line.

My head continues to pound. I retreat beneath the blankets, teasing a couple more hours of sleep from the morning before the phone rings again, waking me from my slumber. I begrudgingly answer the call.

"Hey Sheela! It's me, Sister Webb. I just wanted to let you know I'm heading to the church to set up for this evening's meeting. Come early to help me get the newsletters passed out, okay?"

"Yes ma'am. I'll see you in a few hours" I say as I disconnect the line and climb out of my bed.

The smell of crispy bacon gets my morning started. I chug a small glass of orange juice while preparing my toast and jam.

I'm startled as the entry door to the guest house swings open. Pastor Webb slowly walks inside. Taking a seat on the couch, he crosses his leg at the knee and reclines while watching me.

"Make anything for me?" he asks while grabbing a book from the table.

"I didn't expect company this morning, Pastor Webb, but I'll definitely cook you something if you like."

I open the refrigerator door, but turn to look at him for a response.

"If you don't mind." he says sweetly with a smile.

He removes his leather sandals and places his manicured feet up on the table. His casual shorts extend to cover his thighs as an unbuttoned floral shirt rests on his chest. He adjusts his gold-rimmed frames, moistening his lips with his tongue and watching me for a while before engaging in conversation.

"There's something about you Sheela, I just can't put my finger on it."

Pastor Webb strokes the hairs on his face.

"What do you mean?"

I turn to look at him not knowing how he'll respond.

"I knew your momma. You both have it; that magnetism. It's in your eyes, you draw people in. Even though that may not be your intention, people are attracted to you Sheela. Do you know the responsibility that comes with that?"

Pastor Webb looks seriously in my direction.

"I'm figuring it out, but it's hard to keep all of this to myself when I love to share." I reply as I turn to look at him.

His expression changes and the room is silent except for the popping of frying bacon.

"For we all have sinned and fallen short of the glory of God, but why would you tempt others to sin Sheela?"

Pastor Webb stares, anticipating my answer.

"If God is love, shouldn't he want us to make love? I ask while removing his bacon from the pan and looking flirtatiously over my shoulder at him.

"Yes, but the Bible says we should flee from sexual immorality."

Pastor Webb sits at attention and drops his feet onto the floor.

"The Bible also says that a man commits adultery as soon as his eyes look at a woman in lust." I remind him as I walk towards him.

Wearing only a nightshirt several inches above the knee, I present his breakfast to him in my extended hand.

His eyes are fixed on the fullness of my thighs as he accepts the plate and stands to leave.

"Lord have mercy, let me get out of here."

Pastor Webb laughs to himself and walks to the door.

After the door closes, I think to myself, maybe he'll knock next time.

Returning to bed with my breakfast, I eat slowly and take a moment to ponder my conversation with Pastor Webb.

The sound of the water trickling into the outside pool relaxes me. I cuddle against the plush blankets. The air smells fresh and sweet, not at all like my grandmother's house. I love the way my feet feel as they softly tip across the hardwood floor to the window.

Green fans of palm leaves sway in the wind. I admire how the beautiful color stands out against the crisp blue sky. I open the apartment door and a soft breeze hits my face as I return to sit on the couch, enjoying the view.

I resign to the thought there is no better place than here

and no better man to heal than Pastor Webb.

Pulling my momma's book from below the seat cushions, I take some time to flip through the pages and consider what I should try next. I've been craving chocolate covered strawberries, but I wonder if he'll like marijuana with his wine.

Chapter 17

I can tell by the way Sister Jenkings is sitting that she and
Brother Jenkings have had sex. Her legs are loosely crossed,
and she's chosen to allow her skirt to hike above the knee.
She looks a lot more relaxed, maybe a little flirtatious. I
move a wisp of hair behind my ear, trying to listen as she
talks joyfully to Sister Webb, but their whispers quiet as Sister
Brigham stands in the center of the women's circle, grabbing
everyone's attention before speaking.

"Thank you ladies for being on time. Let's praise God
for that." she says, waving her hands in a dramatic gesture.

"Today Sisters, we will focus on gratitude. We are all so
blessed and have so much to be thankful for. It's good for
everyone to share a celebratory testimony once in a while."

Sister Brigham takes her seat as she nods toward Sister
Webb who happily accepts the floor.

"Amen Sisters! I'm grateful that, although it wasn't under
the best of circumstances, I have Miss Sheela assisting me
for the time being. This girl can cook and y'all know I need
help with that!"

The Sisters nod in agreement with her confession.

"I'll be working with her one on one. Intimacy between
women is so important. I ask that you all keep us in your
prayers.", says Sister Webb, immediately gesturing to me,
inferring it is my turn to share.

The Sisters all turn to look at me as I hold my finger in
the air, buying a few moments of time.

I want to say how grateful I am to have helped Sister Jenkings connect with her husband and how fantastic it feels to finally know my momma through her book. But I knew I couldn't say this out loud.

The recesses of my mind finally reveal a decent answer as I look up and begin to speak.

"I'm grateful for Sister Webb. This is the closest we've ever been. She's welcomed me into her home with open arms. I look forward to serving the Webbs wonderful meals and taking care of whatever else she needs while I'm there. Thank you Sisters for keeping me in prayer."

Everyone smiles and claps their hands with exclamations of Amen as I shrink back into my seat.

Raising her hand, Sister Jenkings enthusiastically volunteers to share as the circle of sisters grows quiet.

"I'm grateful to have the man I married back! About a month ago he came to me and said he was ready to focus on more than just our sex life. He said he'd worked everything out within himself and just wanted to be with me. He's been so patient and attentive. He even started holding my hand again, and I really enjoyed him last night, if you know what I mean." she reveals, giggling to herself.

"It's like he's under a love spell. He can't get enough of me."

Sister Jenkings hides her face bashfully in her hands as she displays the giddiness of a school girl with a crush.

My heart begins to race at the words "love spell" as I suddenly realize the 28 days have elapsed. I recluse into my mind and time is lost as I ponder my affair with Brother Jenkings, wondering if he has been relieved of his feelings for me through sex with his wife. The Sisters continue to

SexMagicFood

share and laugh with one another as I review the pages of my momma's book in my mind, searching for an answer.

I realize the meeting has ended as Sister Brigham grabs my hand and pulls me to stand for closing prayer.

With my head bowed, I hear the conference room door creek open before smelling a hint of cigarettes and Brother Jenkings cologne.

Sister Webb says Amen as the ladies chat and disperse from the circle. Staying in my seat, I pretend to sort papers, not daring to lift my head or turn to look in his direction. I can hear him making small talk with the Sisters. His voice gets louder as he gets closer to me with every brief conversation.

I break into a nervous sweat and can feel the heat from his body as he walks around my chair. Standing uncomfortably close as I look up, making eye contact with him and his wife.

"How've you been Sheela? Sister Jenkings and I went by your grandmother's house with your graduation gift. She said you'd moved out."

Brother Jenkings looks at me with concern.

"I'm good. I'm staying with Pastor and Sister Webb for now." I say, smiling awkwardly at them.

"So, do they let you have visitors or are you locked up for a while." Brother Jenkings inquires.

"I'm not focusing on seeing anyone right now. Just taking time to settle in and show my appreciation to the Webb's."

I'm confused by his questions.

"What about your friends? You just can't forget about them. Keeping a social life is important you know." he says jokingly pushing my shoulder before recoiling.

"Let the girl be. She'll be back out with her friends in no time." Sister Jenkings intervenes, frowning slightly and looking questionably at Brother Jenkings.

"I know, baby, but who is Mr. Tee without the A-Team? She needs to be around people who can lift her up."

Brother Jenkings declares as he turns from her to make eye contact with me.

"You're right. Maybe I'll call Renada to meet up at the drive-in this weekend." I gleefully announce, glancing at him before gently smiling at Sister Jenkings.

"Groovy. I can dig it!" Brother Jenkings says playfully, grabbing my hand before dropping it onto my lap.

"I heard *Invaders from Mars* was a good movie to see. See you around Sheela."

Brother Jenkings prepares to leave, but not before kissing Sister Jenkings and softly gripping her hand as they walk from the conference room.

I've done something wrong, I think to myself.

I can't keep seeing Brother Jenkings if I plan on staying with the Webb's, but I have to fix this. Besides, it's not like having sex with him is a chore or anything, and I do miss the firm grip of his hands.

"You ready, Sheela?" Sister Webb asks, looking exhausted with her purse on her shoulder.

"Let's get out of here."

Sister Webb turns off the lights and encourages me to walk in front of her as we leave the sanctuary.

"You have a nice pair of hips on you, Sheela. Thirty years ago, when I was your age, I had a girlfriend that looked about the same." Sister Webb reminisces while laughing to herself.

"Thanks Sister Webb. You look great, too! I hope I age as well as you.

"You're sweet for noticing. I try to keep my body right.

Have you ever taken a swim at night?", she asks as I pause by my car door.

"Never, but it sounds great!" I say genuinely excited at the possibility of having a little fun.

"Great! Pastor is out of town, so we'll have our own pool party tonight. You bring the snacks and I'll bring the wine. See you at home."

Sister Webb climbs into her coupe and accelerates loudly from the lot.

Chapter 18

The house smells of perfumed candles and two crystal wine glasses sit on the dining room table next to an ice bucket holding a bottle of wine.

"I'll be right down. Just finding us some swimsuits." Sister Webb calls from her bedroom.

"Cool, I'll get started on some snacks."

I walk into the kitchen to survey what's available.

The mood in the house is romantic, and I feel as if I'm preparing for a gentleman as I make the tray of edibles.

A few sliced apples with cheddar cheese are artfully placed on top of crackers and drizzled with honey before I exit the kitchen and stuff the first bite into my mouth.

Bits of apple fall onto the floor as I gasp at the sight of Sister Webb. Her hands are on her hips as she boldly stands in front of me in a one-piece skin toned bathing suit. The fitness of her body shows through the fabric.

"Wow! Sister Webb. I'm shocked, I didn't know... I mean, I never expected..."

I place the tray on the table, hiding my grin as I try not to stare.

"Don't be shy. You can be yourself with me. Here, I got you one too."

Sister Webb smiles as she walks toward me. I'm hypnotized by the movement of her hips and the way her sandals click on the floor as she offers me the small piece of sheer fabric.

"Hurry and go change! I'll grab the snacks and wine and meet you by the pool.", she says, balancing the tray as she walks through the open sliding doors.

After a while in the bathroom, I muster the courage to exit wearing the thin skin toned bathing suit. My hands modestly move across my body as I walk out onto the patio, attempting to hide my exposed breast and thighs.

"Finally!" Sister Webb yells from the pool as I walk onto the patio.

"Grab a drink and let's chat a bit."

I wonder what she has to say as she walks through the water to the shallow end of the pool.

The almost translucent fabric of her swimsuit is soaked with water, and she looks naked under the moonlight. I notice her lean and muscular frame and wonder if she's always been a swimmer. Her hair is neatly tucked under a swim cap and water drips from her skin as she takes a seat on the edge of the pool.

I use a towel to cover my lap and sit on the lounger, feeling shy and out of place, I take a moment to think before recalling her promise to let me know more about Marvin.

Sitting at attention, I fill my wine glass. Holding it in my lap, I take a delicate look at her as she prepares her story.

"Your grandmother had three daughters. Jane Marie was born when she was only 13 and stayed with her father. Your momma and Khaki came much later and really didn't have much of a relationship with their sister. Jane Marie and your grandmother were too much alike to get along.

In the middle of her storytelling, I interrupt Sister Webb.

"Jane Marie, I've seen that name before. I think it was in my momma's..." I stop before saying the word book.

"I'm sorry to interrupt." I say as I look at Sister Webb, encouraging her to continue.

"You see Marvin is Jane Marie's husband, but when they went through a rough patch, something got started between him and your momma. Jane Marie found out about it, but she couldn't keep Marvin away from Sadie. Marvin said he felt as if he were under a spell. He loved Jane Marie more intensely; however he could not stop going back to your mother."

Sister Webb stops and shakes her head as she takes a few steps back into the water.

"I don't know if Marvin is your father, but he left a note on your grandmother's door that caused her great concern."

"Does he think I am his daughter?" I ask.

"He doesn't know for sure. It was something your mother said that he's never been able to let go of. Your grandmother hates him too much to discuss it, but your momma was seeing several men. We're still unsure who started the fire that killed her."

"Wait, so it wasn't Mr. Allen, like my grandmother told me."

I move to the edge of my seat anticipating her answer.

"Sheela, Marvin, is Mr. Allen." she pronounces as she moves further into the water.

"Do you mind if I pour myself another glass? I ask while swallowing the last drop of my wine.

"Take the whole bottle." Sister Webb orders before swimming to the deeper end of the pool.

I recline on the lounge, refilling my glass three times before Sister Webb emerges from the water. I can hear her ask about the music, but my ears are muffled by wine and wandering thoughts.

The sounds of electric piano and a voice singing *I just want to be your lover girl* blasts through the speakers. Jolting me to awareness, Sister Webb pours herself a glass of wine and lies beside me on the lounger. I recoil from her damp skin as her firm, cold thigh touches mine, giving me goosebumps all over.

"I'm sorry, Sheela!" she says, firmly rubbing her hands across my legs before noticeably resting them between my thighs.

"Are you comfortable?"

She speaks flirtatiously as she gently presses her fingers into my skin. My heart races. I can't speak as she continues to rub her hand slowly across my legs. I feel the tenderness of her lips as they softly press against my neck. I tilt my head, allowing her to reach the spot behind my ear.

"Are you comfortable, Sheela?" she asks again in a more sensual manner.

Her lips pause for a moment, awaiting my response.

"You're beautiful, but I've never touched a woman before."

I look nervously at her as she continues to rub her hands across my torso and onto my breasts.

"Well, you've never touched a man before either, right? she asks as she moves to kiss me gently on the chest.

"Right. You know I'm a Virgin." I lie to her as she gently pulls my face toward hers for a kiss.

"How did that feel?" Sister Webb asks while gently recoiling from our kiss.

"Really nice."

I look at her full soft lips before gently leaning in to her.

"Have you ever considered that you may be bi-curious, Sheela?"

I don't have time to respond as her fingers gently touch my face and we exchange another kiss. My tongue slightly enters her mouth before she pulls away.

"Let's go to the water."

Sister Webb smiles and pulls me to a stand.

We quickly tip towards the edge of the pool before she jumps inside, holding my hand and pulling me in behind her. The water splashes as I hit the surface and rise from the depths, letting out a suffocated scream. My soaked curly tresses of hair dangle in front of my face as I playfully splash water in her direction.

"You could have warned me!" I yell as she sprints to the other side of the pool.

"Now, where's the fun in that Sheela?"

She laughs from a distance. "You know how to keep a secret right?" she asks, looking seriously for a moment as the water calms.

"Yes, I can keep a secret."

I slowly walk to her as she disappears below the water.

I can feel waves beneath the surface as she swims to me, grabbing my legs from beneath the water and pulling herself to a stand. She looks at me with lonely eyes as the water runs down her face.

"Tell me what you need" I ask as she wraps her fingers around mine.

"I need to be myself." she declares, kissing firmly into my mouth and backing me onto the side of the pool.

She explores my body with her fingers, softly kissing my breasts and licking my nipples before grabbing my hips and turning me to face the wall.

My hands hold the edge of the pool as she fondles my

breasts, gripping them while sliding her other hand around my body and down my torso. Her fingers move slowly between the snuggly fit fabric of the swimsuit to touch my body. I gasp when I feel the warmness of her hand cuff around me. A tingling sensation fills my body as she moves her hand into position.

Her fingers spread, opening me to the coolness of the water as she strokes her fingers up and down. My body convulses, responding to the intense sensation of pleasure. Arching my back and moaning while resting my head against her. She continues to gently work her fingers deeper inside me, quickly finding the spot and pulsing against it firmly.

The music is just loud enough to hide my moans as she curls her fingers inside, making me cum once, twice, then once again. My hands grip the side of the pool as I ride the waves of ecstasy, but I lose my balance, dizzy and weak as she catches me, turning me around to face her. I barely notice the way she kisses me softly as I recover.

"How do you feel? Bi-curious maybe?"

Sister Webb giggles softly while adjusting my suit.

"I can definitely see myself being curious with you...while I'm here. How do you feel?" I ask, still enjoying her touch.

"Better. More like myself."

She grabs my hand to escort me from the pool. We sit on the loungers and I watch her dry her body as I do the same. Struggling to finish, I fall back onto the seat, still feeling weak and heavy from the water.

"I never thought I would feel this again. God works in mysterious ways." Sister Webb reveals as she lies down behind me, pulling me close as we look up at the stars.

"Tell me about it." I say in agreement as we relax together, falling asleep under the moonlight.

Chapter 19

The theatre lot is dark except for the light from the movie screen. I slowly maneuver my car to an area close to where Brother Jenkings' Cadillac Deville is parked. He eagerly flashes his lights as I pull into the lot and anxiously watches me park my car.

I can feel the pressure from his stare as I take a moment to mentally review my plan. The nurse's simulation room is set with herbed chocolate and candles for our session, but my nerves are racked by thoughts of being exposed before I can make things right with my spell. My stomach grows nauseous as guilt takes its toll.

I'm devastated that I left our bond open. I know he has fallen in love with me. My body can feel him obsessing. It's even worse now that the time has elapsed. I wonder if he feels it too. I wonder if this is what my momma did to Marvin.

I use my jacket to shield my face as I jog towards Brother Jenkings' car. My hands shake nervously as I slowly open the door and slide into the passenger seat. I say hello as he grabs my arm, pulling me into the car. My other arm slams the passenger door behind me.

I utter a few words, trying to explain my plan as he places me on his lap. His hands grip my thighs before gliding up my torso to wrap around me. Gripping the back of my head and gently pulling my hair as his lips eagerly explore my chest. My back slides across the firm leather seats as he gently lays between my legs, kissing my neck as he grinds against me.

Pressing firmly, I feel his manhood become harder as his hands rush towards his waistband.

"Listen. We can't do this here. I have a place."

He continues to loosen his pants. His bare skin touches mine and his fingers slide my panties to the side as he prepares to enter me.

"Listen!" I say grabbing his arms and stopping his effort.

"It's only five minutes from here." I say, looking at him and relieved as the weight of his body slowly lifts from mine.

"Where's this place at?"

"It's my old classroom, it will be vacant for a while. I got it all set up for us."

Brother Jenkings listens as he reluctantly positions himself behind the steering wheel.

"I can dig it. Let's go." he says, impatiently, nodding his head and fastening his pants.

"Follow me there."

I quickly fix my clothes before opening the door and running to my car.

His headlights follow closely behind as we pull from the theatre. Another car appears to be following just as closely as I watch from my rear-view mirror before dismissing the thought, blaming paranoia.

I'm anxious and guilty; my palms are sweaty, slipping against the steering wheel as I turn into the school lot.

I park at the back and use my key to open the door. The scent of cinnamon incense warms the air. I'm relieved to see the herbed chocolate, yellow candle and white linens still in place.

The door swings open as Brother Jenkings impatiently enters the room and locks the door.

"Oh, I see. Good job, baby girl." he says, smiling and rubbing his hands together.

Walking towards me, he grabs my waist and lifts me from the ground. My legs wrap around him as he carries me to the bed and unbuttons my pants. Pulling them from my waist, he kisses softly below my navel.

"Did you miss me as much as I missed you?"

He speaks sensually as he removes everything but his socks, seductively watching me nod in agreement before helping me strip naked.

He runs his hands across my body before entering my vagina. I hold my position, submitting to him as he moans in pleasure, sliding in and out of me. His body convulses, quickly approaching orgasm as I look up at him, hoping to grab his attention.

Warm semen fills my womb as he loses control, moaning loudly while ejaculating and collapsing on top of me. Drawing closer to hug me tight.

"I love you, Sheela." he whispers into my ear.

My heart races and vomit enters my throat. I kiss him quickly while shaking him, encouraging him to rise from my body.

A pair of headlights flicker through the window, reflecting from the wall as I quickly grab the yellow candle and retreat behind the heavy curtain surrounding the bed.

"I'm sorry, Sheela, but would it be so bad? I've always wanted to be a father." Confessess Brother Jenkings.

My heart wrenches at the sound of love in his voice as I hide behind the curtain, squatting over the candle. His semen plops onto the wick and I light it before quickly whispering the love spell.

"Our bond is broken, tonight was only nice. Now return with this love to your wife."

I repeat three times before revealing myself from behind the curtain, relieved to see Brother Jenkings fully dressed and walking to the door.

"Alright Sheela, that was nice. I'm going to go home to my wife."

With this declaration, he opens the door. Not looking back as it closes behind him.

Anxious energy leaves my body as I clean the space, covering everything in plastic and buffing out the marks in the stainless steel.

I toss the stained sheets and exhausted candle in my trunk, smiling to myself as I start my car and drive toward the Webb's.

I adjust my rear-view mirror to look at the lonely pair of headlights behind me. Grandmother always said people get nervous when they ain't living right.

Chapter 20

Arriving at the guest house, I run to the shower. The smell of Brother Jenkings cologne rinses from my body as water pours over my head. I hide my tears, wishing I had my Momma to talk to, or even my father. I try to imagine their faces. Feeling lonely, I watch drips of water bounce from the floor of the tub.

"Hey Sheela, it's me."

I'm startled to hear Renada yell as she jiggles the locked bathroom door.

"Hey, I'll be right out." I respond, quickly exiting the shower.

Growing concerned and wondering why she would come so late and unannounced. I hurry from the bathroom, securing my robe and leaving puddles of water along the floor as I run to her.

"What's going on?" I ask with a tight embrace before stepping back.

"Where have you been? Sister Webb said you were supposed to be at the movies with me, so I went to look for you, but you weren't there." says Renada, looking disappointed and frustrated.

"So that was you following me?" I asked.

My face grows hot with embarrassment as I prepare to be exposed.

"No! I've been here for over an hour waiting for you." she expresses with her voice shaking as she cries.

"It's like you've completely changed. You're lying to

people and I feel like I don't even know you anymore." she says, wiping away angry tears.

"I'm sorry, Renada. I needed to get away and I used you as an excuse. I should've called you and let you know. Please forgive me.", I say humbly reaching for her hand.

"Fine, but where did you go, Sheela? Where have you been all this time?"

Renada lifts her hands and shrugs her shoulders in my direction.

I stare back at her, hesitating to respond, unable to dig up a decent lie from my mind.

"You know what? It's none of your business. I'm grown." I say in a defiant tone as I cross my arms.

"You're really proving your grandmother right, Sheela. I'm starting to wonder about you. Even Christian has stopped coming to your defense."

"What do you mean I'm proving my grandmother right?" I cut my squinting eyes in her direction.

"It's the way you move, Sheela. Christian told me what you said to Brother Marcus, and now you're out late at night with no one knowing where you are! You need to be careful. You don't want people to think you're fast and start calling you a whore!", Renada yells, flinging her arms in wild gestures as she explains her point.

"Fuck what people think! Why should I care about the opinion of a bunch of hypocrites who don't even like me!"

I yell at Renada, feeling betrayed by Christian and wanting her to disappear.

"Well, what about my opinion. Where were you?

Renada stares at me in wait of an answer.

"And don't you dare zone out on me, Sheela!" Renada

snaps her fingers to get my attention.

"I'm tired of this, if you want to call me tomorrow you can, but I can't be around you right now.

I point towards the door as my way of telling her to leave.

"So you're asking me to leave without telling me where you've been?"

Renada crosses her arms and stares at me with insistence.

"I'm asking you to be a friend and give me space without judging." I plead.

Renada puts up her hands in surrender, walking quickly to the door and flinging it open before slamming it closed.

I'm startled by the simultaneous ringing of the telephone. Looking towards the main house as I answer, I see Sister Webb gesture to me from the window.

"Is everything okay?" she asks.

"Yeah, Christian is just spreading his anger over to Renada. We probably won't be speaking for a while."

I try to remain calm although I am full of emotion, trying to catch my breath.

"That's too bad. Do you need me to come cuddle with you?" Sister Webb says sympathetically as we exchange giggles.

"I'm fine. Do you like chocolate-covered strawberries? I'm making some tomorrow night and figured you and the Pastor would enjoy them with some champagne." I ask while looking at my momma's book.

"Now that sounds sexy and delicious. You must have caught wind of our anniversary. I'll put a little extra with the grocery budget. Let's make it a night to remember!"

Sister Webb sounds hungry and excited as we disconnect the line.

I watch from my window as Pastor Webb quickly approaches her. He looks upset and they exchange a heated moment before disappearing from my view.

I open a window to enjoy the cool breeze and take a moment of peace before removing the last marijuana joint from my bag and pouring myself a glass of wine.

I embrace the aroma, thinking fondly of my Aunt Khaki before lighting the end and inhaling the sweet smoke into my lungs. The high carries me above my issues and to an epiphany. I consider using sex to put a spell over the Webb's, healing their marriage while bonding us as a family.

Clouds of smoke exit the window as I ponder the 28 days to follow and the complexities in our relationship it would cause.

It feels selfish, but there's no other place for me. They're all I have now, I need them to need me.

Chapter 21

A bead of sweat starts on my brow as I plead my case. My facial expression is worried as my Aunt Khaki pops her gum, looking unimpressed.

"What's the difference? Just let me buy it."

I'm pleading desperately waiving $40 in the air, but my aunt is not sympathetic.

"But why do you need so much though"

"Because, I want to have enough weed brownies for the party."

I try to sound as convincing as possible, whining in my attempt to look serious.

"Girl! If you don't shut your lying ass up! Whose party are you going too?"

My Aunt Khaki knows the game and scoffs while dismissing me with a hand gesture.

"Aunt Khaki, please, you know this is hard for me. I don't want to look like a dope fiend, but I need you to sell me some weed."

I laugh as I put up my hands in prayer.

"I guess. But you're gonna have to find another plug after this. Momma would kill me if she knew."

Khaki looks concerned as she measures the marijuana before placing it in a bag and handing it to me.

"Thank you! You're the best."

I give her a big hug around her waist before turning to walk through the door.

"Yeah, whatever. Let me know when you're ready to talk about it."

Her suspicious tone stops me in my tracks.

"Talk about what?" I ask, looking over my shoulder at her, my breath becoming short.

"You think I wouldn't notice? You ain't no virgin anymore, Sheela. I ain't blind. But don't worry, your secret's safe...for now. Come back and see me soon, you hear?"

Aunt Khaki smiles and waves me out the door.

I giggle nervously, troubled by her observation, but continue walking. I'm happily distracted by the weight of the marijuana in my pocket.

"Okay see you later. I've got a lot of shopping to do."

I feel her stare as I climb into my car.

I drive with caution, pulling into the Webb's estate, wishing someone would help as my overloaded trunk bounces open again. I slowly cross several speed bumps, watching through my rear-view mirror as groceries and toiletries are tossed into the air. I'm thankful as the able-bodied security guard begins to follow closely behind in his cart, graciously helping me carry everything inside the house.

Finishing up, he refuses a tip, smiling and winking his eye before heading back to his cart.

I kick off my shoes and run into the kitchen, unpacking while contemplating my night with the Webb's. I retrieve the dinner pots, filling one with water before reaching for my mommas book. I take a deep breath and flip through the pages before being startled by the slamming of the front door. The walls vibrate as the force echoes through the house.

Fearful to leave the kitchen, I hide from view just as I hear Pastor Webb yelling in anger.

"You ain't getting no divorce! You knew what this was when you signed the dotted line. Till death do us part!"

Sounding angry, Pastor Webb's heels click swiftly towards the stairwell.

"You're fucking that girl from the store and you're steady trying to deny it! I heard you make another date with her, you stupid son of a bitch! I was listening from the other aisle."

Sister Webb confronts him as her pace quickens in his direction.

Pastor Webb turns to walk up the stairs but not before throwing one last dagger.

"Look at you. Using such foul language, and you wonder why God won't bless your food."

"Fuck you! You're just upset I caught you being a trick. It's a shame when you got all this at home."

"Now you know you went cold on me a long time ago."

Pastor Webb's dismissive tone carries down the stairwell.

"You know what I struggle with. I already need extra encouragement, so I certainly can't get turned on when things aren't right between us."

Sister Webb emphasizes her point by clapping her hands in unison with her words.

"Yeah, I know your struggles. I thought your recent transgression would have soothed your appetite, but it seems you're still jealous that I'm the one with the dick."

Pastor Webb laughs as he starts back up the stairs.

"I hate you! I can't believe I'm stuck with such a narcissistic bastard!"

In frustration and anger, Sister Webb takes off her shoe

and hurls it towards the staircase.

"No, you're the bastard, remember?" says Pastor Webb, his voice moving further away.

Sister Webb cries, uttering a few inaudible words before being interrupted by Pastor Webb.

"Quit trippin'. God made Eve for Adam. I'm not going anywhere, and neither are you. Figure your shit out and I'll keep myself busy."

I hear him lightly jog up the stairway as the heavy click of Sister Webb's heels approach the kitchen.

The pot of water boils over, spilling onto the flame. I hurry to calm the fire as Sister Webb joins me in the kitchen. I toss a towel over my momma's book before turning to address her.

"Don't worry, I won't burn the house down." I say, laughing awkwardly while wiping water from the stove.

"You might as well. It's already hell for me."

Sister Webb begins to cry as she presses her back against the wall.

"I'm sorry. I know how you feel."

My eyes fill with emotion as I try not to think about my grandmother's house.

"Well, I've got a splendid dinner planned for us. Salmon Croquettes with herbed potatoes and asparagus, fresh yeast rolls and chocolate-covered strawberries for dessert. I also grabbed your favorite wine.", I say hoping to change the mood in the room.

"That sounds great Sheela. I'm sorry you had to hear that. We're not used to having people around."

Sister Webb turns slowly to walk from the kitchen.

My heart sinks, and the house is completely silent as the door to her bedroom closes. I stand alone in the kitchen, doubtful, but desperate.

If they won't bond with me, they won't heal and if they can't heal, I can't stay and I have nowhere to go, other than back to my grandmother's.

Beginning to unconsciously pace the kitchen floor, I'm panicked at the thought of being sent away.

Nervously yanking the towel covering my Momma's book, I hurry to find the recipe for herbed butter. The mixture approaches the top of the pot as I intentionally add more cannabis than called for. My heart pounds as I decide to over intoxicate the Webb's, but my mind worries that I won't have the chance to succeed.

Chapter 22

I season fresh Salmon with lemon pepper and the herbed butter before placing it in the oven to bake. My head spins, feeling high as the potent smell of herbs fills the kitchen. I quickly open a window and return to my work.

My eyes lock with focus as my knife knocks against the cutting board. Perfectly quartered potatoes and trimmed asparagus drop into baking dishes as I treat them with savory seasoning and plenty of butter.

I check the time, relieved to be on track as the double boiler steams. Unconcerned with using the proper tools, my eyes measure the chocolate as I pour it into the bowl. I mix in several spoonfuls of herbed butter before nervously looking at Momma's book for a spell.

"Warning: Be certain you have mastered the 28-day cycle and released all suitors before beginning group healing work..." I read quickly, short on time and feeling only slightly detoured as I continue.

> *"Group bonds are momentous and dynamic, making them creative and unbreakable. They become more intense as the 28-day cycle comes to a close..."*

As I read aloud, I impatiently skip ahead several pages to the spell. Finding it, I hold the book in my hand, continuing to stir the chocolate as I speak.

> *"Goddess of the sweet waters, infuse these sa-*

*cred herbs with orgasmic bonds. Allow your magic
to wick into the chocolate and be made whole as it
cools around the passionate red berry. All who eat,
are immediately and shall remain bonded."*

I exhale as I finish the spell and hide Momma's book
beneath the towel.

I carefully select nine succulent strawberries and drench
them with herbed chocolate before placing them in the refrigerator to cool.

I feel satisfied as delicious aromas travel through the
house. The food is moved to serving platters and carefully
arranged before being set on the dinner table. I smile as I
hear rustling footsteps on the upper floor and Sister Webb's
door creeping open.

"Dinner will be served in 15 minutes." I yell through the
quiet halls before escaping to the guest house to get cleaned
up.

Through my window, I can see Pastor Webb approach
the dinner table, holding a folded newspaper in his hand and
trying not to look at Sister Webb as she seats herself. She immediately pours herself a glass of wine, sipping it and looking
away as he reads his paper.

Determined to get them in the mood, I coax the white dress
with golden embellishments from the corners of my bag and
pull it over my head. The material clings to my curves as I
adjust the fabric in my mirror.

I hurry back to the main house, taking a few moments
to prepare myself before dramatically bursting through the
doors.

"Happy Anniversary!" I yell as I joyfully entered the
dining room.

Walking towards the dinner table to hug and kiss the Webb's, Sister Webb attempts to touch my thigh as I take my seat. Thankfully, Pastor Webb, too busy preparing to eat, doesn't notice.

We bow our heads in prayer as delicious warm aromas creep into our noses. There's barely an "Amen" before Pastor Webb cuts into the crunchy croquette. Humming in delight as his fork delivers each savory bite.

Sister Webb smiles while finishing her potatoes.

"You certainly can cook Sheela." she says, shaking her head at me before moving to devour the crisp asparagus.

"What's that flavor? I recognize it but I can't put my finger on it." asks Pastor Webb, looking at a bit of croquette on his fork.

"Herbed butter. It's my momma's recipe."

I nervously stand to pour him a glass of wine.

"Absolutely delicious!"

Sister Webb sips her wine while continuing to take large bites of food.

"I'm so glad you like it! Don't forget I have dessert.", relieved that I see their posture become more relaxed.

"This wine is nice too."

For the first time during the evening, Pastor Webb speaks to Sister Webb. They exchange a reluctant glance before she smiles, nodding her head in response.

"I'll be right back."

I excuse myself to the kitchen, excited to return with the tray of chocolate-covered strawberries.

The Webb's, over intoxicated by the food, become silent and contemplative. They watch me as I place the tray in the center of the table, taking one for Sister Webb.

The air is full of sexual tension as I offer her a taste. She parts her lips, biting into the herbed dessert while staring into my eyes. She licks her lips as I touch her face; she kisses me, and I enjoy the tenderness of her lips before Pastor Webb leaves his chair to join us.

I can feel his hand on my back as he kneels on the ground between us, stroking our legs as he shares our kiss and guides me onto the table.

I stop to feed a chocolate-covered strawberry to Pastor Webb, feeling weightless as Sister Webb kisses my neck. Pastor Webb's fingers move up my dress, expertly removing my underwear. I feel his lips press against my inner thigh as the doorbell begins to persistently ring.

"Who would be here at this hour?"

Pastor Webb grumbles to himself, annoyed as he walks towards the front door.

Sister Webb and I adjust our clothes, sitting and looking innocent as the front door swings open.

"Good Evening Pastor Webb, I'm sorry to bother you so late but I really need to speak to Sheela."

I hear a woman's voice say, confused and hoping it wasn't my grandmother.

"Ok. Come on in Sister Jenkings." says Pastor Webb, confused and squinting his eyes at her.

"Sheela, do you mind if I talk to you over here for a minute?"

Her expression stoic as she gestures to me to leave the table.

Heavily intoxicated, I hold my composure, assuring the Webb's that everything is fine and only stumbling once as I follow her out of view into the sitting room.

Sister Jenkings takes a deep breath, allowing her suppressed anger to come to the surface as she stares at me. Rage fills her eyes and I feel anxiety rush through my body, knowing what she does next could ruin everything. My posture becomes more serious as I mentally prepare.

"So, what have y'all been doing, Sheela!" asks Sister Jenkings.

"Well, I just finished serving dinner. We were about to head to bed." I respond, nonchalantly shrugging my shoulders.

"You know what I'm talking about, Sheela. Tell me what you and my husband were doing last night. I followed you so don't try to lie."

"He didn't tell you?"

I calmly ask, my heart pounding through my dress as I cross my arms.

"Tell me what happened, Sheela! I saw you sitting in his Cadillac before driving to your nursing school."

Although Sister Jenkings is whispering, I can tell by her tone she is filled with anger.

"I never met with Brother Jenkings. I've actually been dating someone from school." I whisper, attempting to look earnest as my voice nervously trembles.

"Quit lying Sheela! I know my husband's car, you fucking whore!"

Sister Jenkings lunges toward me before regaining composure and pulling me further into the room.

"Look, I met up with someone, but it wasn't your husband. I swear. I'm sorry you guys are going through a tough time."

My eyes well with tears as I look apologetic at Sister Jenkings.

"Bitch! I saw him leave before you! Keep on lying Sheela."

Sister Jenkings is becoming increasingly frustrated.

"Why don't you ask him? "

I try to soften my voice which is anxious with emotion.

"I can't. I'm afraid. He's so good to me, I just can't go accusing him of... Just tell me what you did!"

Sister Jenkings pushes me onto the sofa just as the severely intoxicated Webb's reveal their hidden position behind the doorway.

"Hey now! This sounds like a misunderstanding. The girl already told you she didn't see him. Why don't you make your way home, Sister Jenkings? I'm sure he's worried sick about you."

Pastor Webb, firmly patting Sister Jenkings on the back, guides her out the door.

The lock clicks behind her as I stand in the foyer with the Webb's, looking mortified before laughing hysterically. Following my lead, Pastor Webb holds his stomach, barely able to breathe as he laughs into the wall.

"I told you to be careful, Sheela. There's a downside to being good looking. Anyway, I gotta go lay down."

Pastor Webb turns to leave as he chuckles to himself.

"Mind if we join you?", I ask, winking and grabbing Sister Webb's hand.

"Of course not! Let's go!" he says, grinning and motioning for us to hurry.

I hurry to grab the strawberries and quickly meet them at the stairs. We're already beginning to stroke each other as we walk into Pastor's luxurious bedroom.

He closes the door behind us as I bend at the waist, extending my arms to grip the wall.

I hold steady, standing on my toes and extend my ass while

patiently waiting for my lady and gentleman.

The warmth I'd prayed for overtakes me as they caress my body. We make love, bonding our destinies, as the halls echo with our moans until the morning.

Chapter 23

I can feel them all the time. Everyone is calm now, but they'll need me soon. It's been several months and many clandestine nights since we began, but I still get nervous. There is excitement in feeling Brother Jenking's infatuation and the Webb's desire to bond so closely together. They don't know about each other; all they know is they're mine.

I'm no longer afraid to admit, I too am becoming wrapped up in their love, hopelessly trapped under the warmth of their caresses. I'm jealous when their affection lacks, so I respond by strengthening the power of my spell with each monthly session.

I keep them all comfortable. Staying available and always ready to be filled with love or covered in sweet sticky desire. They're always happy, so they do their best to keep me happy.

Together, the Webb's have turned the modest guest house into a home fit for a princess. All the finest clothing hangs in my wardrobe and they have upgraded the furniture to something more plush and permanent.

Every 28 days I receive a bouquet of yellow roses from Brother Jenkings with our meeting place written on the card. He never fails to disappoint, reserving only the best rooms and arriving late only once because of Sister Jenkings' suspicion. Although we're much more careful, she still ignores me during service.

Tonight, he wants to meet up at a kickback on the more artsy side of town. He says he wants to get away, get lost in the big city, or maybe pretend there's nowhere else to be.

I share the best parts of him with Sister Jenkings, and he's a good friend, but I can't help feeling disappointed that I can't have a love for myself.

Through the guest house window, I can see the Webb's dancing to what must be one of their favorite songs. Pastor Webb swings Sister Webb gently away from him, spinning her around then holding her close. In trance and in love, they stare into each other's eyes. I watch longingly, anticipating my invitation to join them after tomorrow night's dinner.

I dry cleaned my yellow polka dot romper for tonight. Brother Jenkings hasn't seen it since the first time we met at the movies. Maybe he'll cum on himself again. I'm sure he could with my help.

The stretchy fabric snaps onto my body as I toss my long, silk pressed curls over my shoulder. A coat of red lipstick compliments my red heels and I admire myself in the mirror before quickly grabbing my bag and heading towards the door.

Brother Jenkings asked me to meet him at 9:00 p.m. I don't like to keep my gentleman waiting.

I arrive at the luxury condominium complex with 15 minutes to spare. There are grand balconies at almost every level and the lobby is nicely decorated in gold, white and clear glass. There is a happy dispositioned concierge smiling at me from the front desk when I enter.

"Excuse me, sir. I'm looking for apartment number 924. I've never been here before and I'm meeting a friend." I say, timidly walking towards him.

"You're the tenth person to ask for that apartment in the last hour. You guys are going to have a blast. Follow the sign to the elevator and then go up to the ninth floor. It will be the fifth apartment on your left."

The concierge continues to smile as I thank him and make my way to the elevator.

My heart pounds as I knock on the door to the party, only now realizing I may not fit in. The door is opened by a beautiful Indian woman wearing a studded leather jacket and cut-off shorts. Her bra is exposed, but slightly covered by the long tresses of straight hair over her shoulders.

"I'm Lanette, who the fuck are you?" she boldly inquires as she returns her cigarette to her lips and looks me up and down.

"Hey Lanette, I'm Sheela. I'm meeting a friend here by the name of Jenkings, I'm here a little early."

I hope my respectful tone helps me gain entry.

"Who the hell is Jenkings? Fuck it, it doesn't matter, come on in. We'll make the proper introduction once the mutha fucka shows up."

Lanette pulls me into the apartment and closes the door.

The music is loud, and the air is hazy in the small yet open apartment. All of the eclectic furniture has been moved to one side of the space, exposing what looks like polished concrete floors under the dim light.

A few purposeful guests cluster together, sharing bongs and yelling deep philosophical anecdotes over the noise. Others, more heavily intoxicated, dance without inhibition in the center of the room. Everyone seems to be unbothered by the couples who find refuge in the dark corners, kissing and touching as if no one was around.

I grab a beer from an open cooler, feeling lost as I awkwardly traverse the crowded apartment, hoping to see a familiar face. The isolation of the balcony seems more welcoming as I look for the marijuana joint in my bag. Comforted as I carefully place it between my fingers and open the door.

"Brother Marcus, what are you doing here?" I say, dropping the beer and hiding the joint.

Butterflies fill my stomach as my heart almost leaps from the balcony.

"My, my, my Sheela Diggs. Don't you look fine tonight."

Brother Marcus is softly biting his lip and shaking his head as he gazes from my hair to my toes.

The familiar scent of his soft cologne is already intoxicating me, and I can't help but notice the way moonlight reflects off his smooth chocolate skin. I've been waiting for him and now, in this moment, alone with him, where no one can see, I can tell he's been waiting too.

"I haven't seen you at church since your divorce. I'm sorry that you and Sister Marcus couldn't work things out."

"Yeah, I had to get away from church for a bit. There are too many connections and old memories there. I'm in a much better place though. Kind of wishing I would've done it a long time ago." he comments, shrugging his shoulders before pulling a joint from his cigarette case and lighting it.

"Do you mind if I hit that?" I ask as I place my joint back into my bag.

I remove the joint from his fingers and take a couple of puffs before passing it back to him. Our fingers lightly touch as he takes it and continues to look out into the sky.

"So, who do you know here?" he asks, releasing smoke from his lungs.

"One of my friends from school told me about this party and then bailed on me. I was so happy to see a familiar face. I could've jumped for joy when I saw you."

I laugh as I flirtatiously rub his arm.

"I have to admit that I was pretty happy to see you as well. I was invited, but I just haven't been able to jive."

Brother Marcus thumps ash into the corner and takes another puff of the joint.

"Do you mind if I stand a little closer to you? It's getting a little chilly out here, but I'm not quite ready to go inside yet." I ask, shivering and rubbing my arms.

"Sure, only if you don't mind the scent of day-old cologne mixed with marijuana."

Brother Marcus laughs as he passes the joint back to me.

"Believe it or not, it's one of my favorite scents. Especially when it's coming from you."

I move closer and intentionally graze his torso with my shoulder.

"You always smell like vanilla and honey." Brother Marcus comments, displaying an enormous grin across his face.

"Wow! You know how I smell? I didn't even think you noticed me." I say, covering my mouth as I gaze at him.

"You're pretty hard to miss, Sheela. Anyone who says they didn't see you come in here is lying. You're impossible not to notice."

Brother Marcus gives me a side eye as he takes the joint from my fingers.

"No, you're the one who's impossible, but I like a challenge."

I move even closer and allow his hand to skim my ass.

"Be careful, Sheela. It's been a while. I may just try to take advantage.

"Let's find somewhere for you to do just that."

I face him and glance below his waist.

Brother Marcus tilts his head back, letting out a light chuckle as his hands gently wrap around my waist. He pulls me closer to him and I close my eyes, preparing for a kiss.

"Jenkings, is that you?"

Brother Marcus breaks the mood with a surprised look as he sees Brother Jenkings standing in the open entrance to the balcony.

I turn around, also looking stunned that I'd somehow forgotten about Brother Jenkings. He seems to be destroyed by the way Brother Marcus gently holds me against his body. His hand stroking the rippled fabric of my romper.

"Yeah, it's me, man. Shit, what are you doing here? Do you know Lanette or something?" Brother Jenkings asks, clearing his throat and nervously pulling a cigarette from his case.

"Yeah, that was a little thang I used to do, but we're just cool now. Hell, I was surprised as fuck to see Sheela here. The way it's looking we might chop it up and head out soon."Brother Marcus announces as he leans down to kiss my cheek.

Feeling the tenderness of his lips on my face for the first time, I unconsciously smile and relax into his embrace. Only briefly unaware of Brother Jenkings agony.

"Wait a minute man, you and Sister Marcus ain't been separated long enough for all that."

Brother Jenkings laughs awkwardly as he takes hard pulls from his cigarette, continuing to watch Brother Marcus's hands molest my romper.

"And Sheela, what are you doing here?", Brother Jenkings quickly asks, smiling and trying not to look jealous.

"I got stood up by a friend and found Brother Marcus out here. It's good to see you though."

I return the smile and mouth my silent apologies.

"It's good to see you too, and in a yellow romper no doubt. I can dig it."

Brother Jenkings, looking depressed as he extinguishes his cigarette, walks over to give me a quick hug.

"Meet me at the door in 30 minutes." he whispers, recoiling from our embrace and staring briefly into my eyes as he reluctantly walks from the balcony.

"See you later, Brother Jenkings." I call out to him as I look down at the large, dark chocolate colored hand covering my torso.

The sweet smell of Brother Marcus's cologne invades my skin as I intentionally press my back against him. He grips me a little tighter, placing another kiss on my neck as goosebumps cover my body. I imagine exposing the bulge between his legs and wrapping my lips around it as I feel it grow larger.

"You still cold?" he asks, softly turning me around to look at my face.

My eyes lock on his tongue as it moistens his lips, and all my inhibitions melt under the weight of my most erotic fantasies as I gently touch his crotch. Staring into his eyes and asking for permission to go further.

"There's no reason to rush Sheela. Now that I'm free, we have time to figure this out."

He winks and finally places his lips to mine.

I refuse to let our first kiss be short as I passionately force him down into the patio chair and straddle his waist. My hands grip his face and I kiss him until I'm satisfied, leaving a trail of red lipstick across his face to his neck.

"Sorry, I've been wanting to do that for a while." I declare, looking relieved as I stand and adjust my outfit.

Brother Marcus silently stares back at me, out of breath, but smiling and shaking his head.

"Oh no! You have lipstick all over you! Let me go grab a napkin."

I laugh as I run towards the door.

"Wait, put this in your pocket before you go."

Brother Marcus reaches into his wallet and hands me a card with his new address and phone number.

I wink at him as I tuck it into my bag and walk back into the crowded space.

Brother Jenkings is already standing by the front door, aggressively motioning for me to join him as I try to return to the balcony with the paper towel. I can feel a dangerous desperateness growing inside of him and decide to leave without telling Brother Marcus goodbye.

Brother Jenkings walks out ahead of me, waiting only a few doors down as I make my way to him.

"What the fuck was that about? So, your fucking Brother Marcus now too?"

Brother Jenkings sounds demanding while firmly grabbing my shoulders to place me against the wall and stare squarely into my eyes.

"No, but I am not married, and I don't belong to you. So just tell me if you would rather me go back home. I'm sure you have better things to do."

I push away from him and start walking down the hallway towards the elevator as he grabs my hand.

"Sorry, blame my jealousy on the fact I've been waiting a fucking month to see you. I also remember that romper."

Brother Jenkings smiles as he recalls the first time I wore it for him, softening the mood.

"Let's go back to the guest house this time. Just follow me through the gate and I'll show you where to park.", I say, pressing the button for the elevator.

Brother Jenkings nods his head in agreement, kissing my hand and pulling me close. The bell rings and the door opens, we step onto the lift. I immediately gasp at my reflection, humiliated by the red lipstick smeared below my chin.

"Oh yeah, I forgot to tell you. You've got lipstick all over your mouth." Brother Jenkings says, remaining slightly tense while clutching me close.

Chapter 24

"Am I your one and only, Sheela?"

Brother Jenkings asks me, moaning while I rub my fingers across his chest and grind back and forth on top of him.

"I am. When you want me."

I look down at him and enjoy the intense tingle caused by his stroke.

I close my eyes as my mind wanders back to Brother Marcus. I moan louder, thinking of him as I rock steadily on top of Brother Jenkings.

"That's it. I like that."

Brother Jenkings grabs my waist as I lift slowly up and down.

"Is that good, Brother Marcus." I whisper, whimpering as tingles surge between my thighs.

Brother Jenkings stops abruptly.

"Did you just call me Marcus?"

"Maybe." I whisper.

Unconcerned with his feelings, I dismount, locking eyes with him as I place his penis in my mouth.

I imagine I'm no longer in my room, but back at the party with Brother Marcus as I lick the shaft of his manhood with my tongue. I can even hear the music as I fantasize, sucking the tip of Brother Jenkings' penis until his legs shake. I taste his semen in my mouth for the first time as he swells to his limit.

"Fuck, I'm about to nut"

Brother Jenkings cries out loudly as his manhood pulses in ecstasy. He grips my hair, and I encourage him as his semen shoots into my throat.

I leave the bed, hurrying to spit his semen over the wick of the yellow candle waiting in my bathroom before lighting it and whispering the spell.

As I return to the bedroom, Brother Jenkings is already dressing and giving his intended response as I take a sigh of relief and prepare to walk him to the door.

"I'll see you at service." I call out to him, whispering loudly as he tips along the stone walk that leads away from the guest house.

My attention turns to my purse as I close the door behind him, tossing random receipts onto the ground as I dump the contents of my bag onto the sofa, excitedly looking for Brother Marcus's card. I suppress sounds of joy as I find it and hold it in my hand.

I pick up the phone, taking a minute to think about the consequences before dialing his number. My heart pounds and I nervously clench my throat, hoping I'll be able to speak.

After only a few rings, Brother Marcus answers and I hear the soft mellow tone of his voice say hello. Speechless, I grin to myself, basking in the glow of finally having him.

"Hello." he says, speaking a little louder.

"Hey, sorry, it's me, Sheela. I'm surprised you answered." I awkwardly laugh into the phone.

"I figured; you're the only person I know who would call me just to zone out."

His laugh calms my nerves.

"Do I zone out?" I ask, sounding embarrassed, but actually flattered that he noticed.

"Yeah, it's kind of cute though."

"Well, maybe it's best that I keep some thoughts to myself. They get kind of nasty when I'm around you."

I smile to myself while waiting for his response.

"Come on, let me know what's on your mind. Who knows, we might be thinking about the same thing."

I recline on the sofa as we continue talking. The jovial sound of his voice is turning me on.

"So, you could see yourself taking things further with me?" I ask, in a seductive voice.

"I can't lie and say I haven't been thinking about you, Sheela. Hell, I'm still wiping lipstick off my chest."

The volume of his laugh fluctuates over the phone as he adjusts his position.

"Yeah, I'm not sorry about that! Do you want to come over so I can finish what we started?"

I giggle as I hear him laugh to himself.

"Dang, shouldn't we wait a few dates before making love? You got me nervous over here."

"Stop playing, I just want to put my lips on you. You can't have my pussy yet."

The mood becomes more sexual and tense.

"You're too much, Sheela."

Brother Marcus laughs but becomes more serious in tone.

"Let's meet up tomorrow. I want you to come see my new place."

I look towards the main house, reminding myself of my commitment to the Webb's, before responding.

"I can't; I'm committed, but we can link up after church this weekend."

As I finish my sentence, I hear a sudden click on the line

which causes me to pull the phone away from my ear.

"Are you there?" I ask, listening for Brother Marcus' response.

"Yeah, I thought that was you. Maybe you've got an eavesdropper." he says, continuing his jovial mood.

"I hope not." I reply as I look towards the main house.

"Oh, well, I better get to bed. See you this weekend." I say, suddenly feeling nervous.

We say our goodbyes as I disconnect the line and stand to move closer to the window.

The once darkened lights of the main house flash on, illuminating the pool as I watch Pastor Webb walk out onto the patio. He paces, appearing to be enraged, before furiously walking to the guest house.

I back up to my bedroom doorway as he barges into the guest house. He looks possessed and in a jealous rage as he charges towards me.

"You sorry ass whore! You trying to fuck the whole church now." he screams as he grabs my neck.

He tightens his grip as I struggle to free myself.

"Please stop, I can't breathe."

I manage to pull at his fingers as his nails pierce my skin.

"You think I didn't see Jenkings leaving my property or hear you on my phone with Marcus? Bitch, you're mine, don't make me kill you to prove it." Pastor Webb roars.

He continues to grip my neck more tightly, pushing me into my room as tears well in his eyes.

I try not to fall, fighting the pressure of his body against my neck, as he forces me onto the bed. My eyes held shut as I fiercely scratch at his arms.

He struggles to keep me pinned, reluctantly releasing me

as I jump from the bed and stumble to a stand. I attempt to run away but he snatches the back of my robe and swings me onto the ground.

I scream in terror as he kneels and places his knees on my arms, repeatedly punching my face with clenched fists until my head aches, and my skin splits with each pound. I hear the unique sound of cracking bones as he repeatedly strikes my jaw and my temples. My vision is tinted red as blood pushes into my eyes.

"Please stop." I cry out softly.

"You brought this on yourself."

Exhausted from the beating, Pastor Webb rises from his stance over me.

I suddenly feel the absence of his weight and hear the jingle of his belt buckle as he stands to remove his pants.

My eyes swollen shut, I kick blindly, landing my foot between his legs and scramble to the open bathroom door as he grabs himself, cursing while reeling in pain.

I lock the door from the inside and fade in and out of consciousness as he bangs on the door. Tiring after several minutes.

"You're not seeing anyone else for a while!" he yells, crying as I hear the front door slam.

The house is quiet as I blindly feel my way into the tub, crying and sitting still as sweat, tears and blood run down my broken face. Anxiety and fear run through my veins as dark blood leaks from my head, filling my swollen eyes. My jaw feels locked, and I'm beginning to feel faint, but I don't dare leave, petrified by light entering the bathroom from the main house.

I reach up and turn on the shower, carefully using cold

water to wash the blood from my face. I'm discouraged by increasing soreness and fatigue, but I fight through, clearing my vision in one eye.

I turn off the water and attempt to stand, but my legs won't move. Blood pours from my gashes and I hear a sweet voice crying for me, calling out my name. My vision goes dark and I collapse into the tub.

As I regain consciousness, I hear several muffled voices in the bathroom. Cold, gloved hands grip my body, pulling me from the tub as I hear my grandmother's voice.

"Jesus! Not again!" she yells, before frantically denying my death.

I can briefly see my Aunt Khaki's face as she fights through the crowd of medics, swinging her elbows and demanding they let her through.

"Oh lord! Imma kill that mutha fucka!" she declares as she lays her eyes on me and turns to charge towards the front door.

"Don't make Sheela's problems any worse, Khaki. You never know what she was up to."

I hear a man say in a stern voice. He speaks as if they are familiar, but I don't recognize him.

"Shut the fuck up, Marvin! Every time yo white ass show up somebody dies. Matter of fact, this is for Sadie."

Aunt Khaki lunges from the bathroom.

I hear violent commotion and moving furniture as she continues to scream at him, cursing him for taking her sister.

Unbothered, the medics position my body on the transport bed, using a sheet and blanket to cover my body as they push through the family drama.

"What if she's using magic like her momma, Khaki? What else would have caused Pastor Webb to beat her like this.

Marvin reasons with Khaki while panting heavily and wiping blood from his lip as the medics carry me past.

"How in the hell?" says my grandmother.

Lost for words as she removes my momma's book of spells from beneath the sofa, turning to look at Aunt Khaki and Marvin, she finds herself in a familiar space.

Chapter 25

I finally have a father. I have to admit, I was surprised to see a white man in a dashiki peering over my hospital bed. Marvin told me I was his daughter and introduced me to Jane Marie, his wife and the Aunt I never knew. She said no one had ever told her about me, but she could understand why, now seeing her husband all over my face.

Grandmother had created an elaborate story about how I survived a nearly fatal car accident to answer the questions about my extended hospital stay. I shutter every time she lies, still feeling pain where Pastor Webb's fist fractured my skull.

Although the Webb's begged for my return, covering all medical bills and expressing sincere regret, my grandmother insisted I come back to her, blaming herself for not burning the book. The Webb's are still unable to understand how things became so distorted, sexual and violent, calling me daily to say they still yearn for me, even in their dreams.

My father confessed everything to me, including that although what he did was horrible, he felt freed after murdering my momma. He said oracles led him to tell me about his act as repentance; it is the only way to break the bonds of the spell outside of death.

—

I prepare myself as the gravel on the church lot crackles beneath my tires. It has been months since I laid eyes on my second home.

As I step inside, strangely excited to smell the familiar scents of the sanctuary, I adjust the skirt of my tightly fitted white dress to the proper length for service before moving closer to the door.

From the hall, I can hear Pastor Webb in the midst of his sermon. I wait for a moment, allowing him to come to a pause before joining the congregation and taking a seat on the back row.

Christian notices me, smiling and placing his hand on his chest as he looks admiringly at my figure. I smile to acknowledge his silent compliment before turning my attention to the pulpit.

"Brothers and Sisters, it says in first John that if we repent of our sins, He is faithful and will forgive our sins and purify us from all unrighteousness."

I watch Pastor Webb reading from his Bible as he addresses the congregation.

"You see, this is a beautiful gift, but you must understand how to repent, lest you confess in vain. Listen carefully, there are five steps..." he pronounces while stopping to allow everyone a moment to prepare.

"First, confess wrongdoing to yourself. Second, testify before your brother and sisters.

Third, ask God for forgiveness. Fourth, turn away from the sin. And, fifth, you must make whole what you have wronged."

Closing his Bible, Pastor Webb continues his poetic delivery from the pulpit.

As the sermon concludes, I muster the courage to repent, now desperate to break the spell. I pray to myself, preparing for humiliation as Pastor Webb delivers the invitation to the altar.

Feedback whistles from his microphone as Deacon Brigham approaches the altar.

"Everybody rise."

Deacon Brigham gestures his hands in an upward motion.

The congregation joins him as he sings a familiar song. Their eyes peeking towards the center aisles as the fallible march towards sinners' row.

I take a deep breath, attempting to contain my nerves as I step from my pew and walk towards the altar, praying with each step for release of the spells that have been anchored to my soul.

The eyes of the congregation stare at me as I take the long walk. Sister Jenkings stands near the end of her row, looking suspiciously through her usual scowl as Brother Jenkings eyes try not to follow me. He fails, looking desperate, obviously starving for my attention.

The Webb's both move to the edge of the stage as I approach, unconcerned with the congregation as they conspicuously stare at me.

I look to my grandmother as she awkwardly mouths threats and gestures for me to join her on the second row. The look of terror in her eyes is a silent plea, discouraging the release of secrets. I turn from her gaze as I reach the altar.

"It's so good to see you, Sister Diggs." says Deacon Brigham, handing me a repentance card.

"It's good to be here.", I say taking the card and looking back to see Grandmother angrily making her way out of the sanctuary.

I feel a warm hand rub across my shoulder as I take my seat. Renada sits beside me and hugs me tight.

"I'm proud of you, Sheela."

Renada bows her head in prayer, encouraging me to write my repentance.

Deacon Brigham approaches the distinguished looking elderly sister sitting to my left. He extends his hand to grab her repentance card. She resists, clenching it in her fist as he snatches it from her hand, causing her to look away in shame.

"Brothers and Sisters, we have Sister Henry here with us today."

Deacon Brigham grumbles as he grabs her arm. They both struggle to remain balanced as he helps her to a stand.

The Sister takes a moment to steady herself before looking into the congregation and removing the microphone from Deacon Brigham's hand.

She attempts to maintain her dignity as feedback whistles throughout the sanctuary, clearing her throat as the apparent awkwardness intensifies.

"Good morning, Brothers and Sisters. Now, I know I've been lying about this for over a decade, but I confess that I stole my potato salad recipe from Sister Brigham. I also put salt in her banana pudding at the last picnic. I ruined it for everybody. I'm sorry. God forgive me. I repent."

The Sister bows her head in shame as she hands the microphone back to Deacon Brigham and returns humbly to her seat.

"Amen, Amen. God is in the healing business."

Deacon Brigham hurries the microphone to me, seemingly in good spirits as I stand to meet him.

"Now, this young lady is a walking miracle." he says, softly grasping my hand.

"Just four months ago she lay broken in a hospital bed, skull fractured, eyes swollen shut and purple with bruises. A

horrible accident almost took her young life and now she's
here to…",

Deacon Brigham stops speaking suddenly, shocked at
reading my repentance.

"Oh no, oh my…."

The Deacon stumbles and stutters. Panicked, he quickly
returns my card before walking toward the exit doors.

"Y'all just never learn!" Deacon Brigham yells.
Dramatically slamming the door behind him.

The Webb's leave the pulpit and place their arms around
me, explaining they need to counsel me in a private room as
an Elder steps forth to continue the program.

The eyes of the congregation follow us as we walk behind
the heavy red velvet curtains and into the nearest conference
room. Pastor Webb gently closes the door and turns to glare
at me.

"Give me that fucking card. What the fuck were you about
to do, Sheela?"

Pastor Webb snatches the card from my hand and reads it
to himself as Sister Webb stands closely behind me.

"Please, I need to repent, it's the only way to free all of
us from this...this...spell. I know you can feel it. You almost
killed me in a jealous rage." I say.

I'm barely able to fight back tears and become emotional
while mentally recalling the severe beating.

"You used sex magic and food to put love spells on us,
Sheela?" Pastor Webb questions.

Reading the card again, he looks relieved.

"Not every time, but once a month I used magic to bond
your marriage, consequently your bond now includes me.
We have to repeat the ritual and spell every 28 days or your

passion for me will become insatiable."

They look at each other as they begin to understand their unexplainable lust.

"So, are you sure repenting will break the spell? You've mentioned Jenkings here too. I think this is too much to disclose in public."

Exhausted, Pastor Webb places his hands over his face while dropping into a chair.

"I have no other option." I say, unwilling to mention death.

"Does Jenkings know about us?" asks Pastor Webb, sitting at attention as he awaits my answer.

"No, you weren't even supposed to know about him.

"Alright, go in there and repent of your sins committed with Brother Jenkings. If it works, we'll fly to a church out of state and resolve our issues there."

Pastor Webb sweats under the pressure of this information.

The room becomes quiet, and sexual tension grows between us as we consider our options.

"Forget it, I'm leaving. I'll figure something out."

I turn to open the door, suppressing the desire to hug them before leaving.

"Wait, what about us?" Sister Webb demands, reaching for me as I move away.

"I've got to go calm my grandmother and then I'll come by tonight. Leave the back gate open for me."

I close the conference room door and tip through the back exit to my car.

I take a moment to stand outside in the parking lot before starting my car. The wind gently blows as I listen to the angelic voice of the congregation singing through the walls of the church. Wishing I could go back to a time when I belonged there, a time not now.

Chapter 26

Everyone is still in service, so my grandmother's street is eerily quiet. As I park in the driveway, I notice there's not a single car in the neighborhood except for ours.

I open her front door and am greeted by a strange silence. Immediately noticing that the lights are dimmed as if no one is home and there are no delicious smells coming from the kitchen.

"Grandmother?" I call timidly through the hallway.

"Girl, don't you yell in my house."

I hear my grandmother say in a commanding tone. She sounds disgusted, so I use caution, walking slowly as she speaks to me from the dark corner in her bedroom.

"Sorry Grandmother, I didn't mean to yell. I was just looking for you."

"Don't you dare come any closer, Sheela." she directs, raising her hand from the shadow.

"My God, your momma left me with such a burden. Your existence itself is an embarrassment. I should have followed my first thought and put you in the ground as a baby."

She speaks insensitively, delivering these shocking statements while rocking faster in her chair.

"I hope your stupid ass had fun ruining my reputation with the church. That was the only thing I had left."

Grandmother confesses, choking with emotion and crying to herself.

I step further into her room, remaining silent and now able

to see that her hand is inside a paper bag, tightly gripping the contents.

"And who told you to take that book. I guess you're a whore and a thief. I tell you, girl, I could just strike you down."

Her voice quivers with anger.

I open my mouth, attempting to explain, but she leaps from her chair and barrels towards me. Pushing me onto the ground and back into the hallway.

"I never wanted you! You're the cursed half breed baby of a witch and all you bring is pain."

Grandmother yells and kicks at my legs as I dodge her blows.

"I didn't choose you either, Grandmother, but at least I tried. I would rather repent and be known as the church whore than to be a narcissistic liar like you."

Climbing from the ground, I walk towards the front door.

I feel the heat of her body on my back and turn around to see her holding a silver .38 caliber handgun. She looks into my eyes as she points it directly at my heart and without saying another word, pulls the trigger.

A loud pop precedes an intense stinging pain in my chest. I drop to the ground, unable to speak. Crying for my momma, I gasp in pain as the blood empties from my body. I look at my grandmother in disbelief as streams of blood turn my white dress scarlet red.

She turns away, leaving me in the doorway as she slowly walks into her room. I hear another loud pop, followed by silence as my eyes fix on the ceiling, a tear rolling down my cheek. I fade out of consciousness as I feel my soul being pulled into the light.

About Amiya Cleveland

Amiya Cleveland was born in 1981 and raised in the infamous Fort Worth, Texas neighborhood known as "Stop Six." An introvert by design, Amiya wasn't allowed to play outside in the dangerous neighborhood named for its "colored only" bus route. Instead, she developed a love of reading and writing in her solitude. Amiya's southern Christian roots and flavor contrast the sexuality and ritualistic practices she envisioned and created for her debut novel, "Sex Magic and Food." In her quest and exploration of the possibilities for those desperate for love, Cleveland plans to publish a series of sequels to Sex Magic and Food," along with accompanying cookbooks on cannabis enchantments.

Made in the USA
Columbia, SC
19 May 2021

38223627R00109